ACHILLES' HEEL

LUKE CHRISTODOULOU

VINCI BOOKS

Vinci Books

vinci-books.com

Published by Vinci Books Ltd in 2026

1

The publisher and the author have made every effort to obtain permissions for any third party material used in this book and to comply with copyright law. Any queries in this respect should be brought to the attention of the publisher and any omissions will be corrected in future editions.

A CIP catalogue record for this book is available from the British Library.

Paperback ISBN: 9781036712631

The EU GPSR authorised representative is Logos Europe, 9 rue Nicolas Poussion, 17000 La Rochelle, France contact@logoseurope.eu

By Luke Christodoulou

Murderous Greece

Pandora's Box
Achilles' Heel
Beware of Greeks Bearing Gifts

Greek Island Mysteries

The Olympus Killer
The Church Murders
Death of a Bride
Murder on Display
Hotel Murder
Twelve Months of Murder

*Dedicated to everyone
struggling with their Achilles' Heel
(Whatever it may be…)*

Part I

INDULGE

Chapter One

ISLAND OF CORFU, GREECE

May, 2022

Out of all the ways a person could wish to be woken up, violent screaming is definitely not one of them. But that was the case for the residents of Saint John's village, just a twenty-minute drive from the town centre of Corfu. Well, at least it was the case for the ones living on the street that led up to Livos Mansion. One by one, they were shaken out of their trip to the abstract lands of Morpheus as the decidedly female shrieks grew louder. Some approached their open windows, pulling back thin curtains dancing upon the night's cool breeze, in search of the person in need. In danger. Some stared at the time in disbelief. A quarter to two. Darkness roamed their once tranquil road, and none dared to venture outside. They were all past their prime, in their late seventies and early eighties, and none desired an encounter with a dangerous robber. The only place with any sign of light was the house on the hill that overlooked

3

their homes. It was a single light, faint and weak, shining alone in the pitch black.

The police station in town received four calls on that spring night concerning the incident, each merely seconds apart.

Lieutenant Damien Levante was at his favorite place when on night call. The infamous Italian-built cabaret on the outskirts of town. 'Cheap drinks, cheap women, close to everywhere in ten minutes,' he would excuse his choice to his disapproving partner. Sergeant Anneta Georgiou would just shake her head and bite her lower lip with her rather large front teeth. 'Whatever you say, boss. I'll be at home in front of my TV, enjoying the miracle of our modern era. Streaming!'

Damien had just ordered his fourth whiskey. 'Just two cubes of ice, this time, Mike. It's the alcohol I'm paying you for, not water.' He spoke without facing the bartender. His eyes were fixated on the dance floor. Bodies wearing the least possible coverings moved around to the euphoric beats provided by the resident DJ. As he brought the cold glass to his parched lips, he felt the vibration in his pocket. Incoming call from the station. He quickly stood up and dashed outside. The cold night air swept off the droplets of sweat that had formed on his wide forehead. He hated the fact that his hairline receded year by year. He despised that next year he was going to hit the big four-zero. At least, he had fewer grey hairs than most of his same-age friends. But they had all married and produced offspring, so a majority of greys was unavoidable according to his theory.

'Hello? Lieutenant Levante here.'

'Sir, we have received multiple calls about screams coming from a house out in Saint John's village. The pinpoint of the location has been texted to you. A unit has just left the station and should be arriving there in fifteen minutes tops.'

'I'll be there in ten,' he replied.

He was inside his Mercedes SUV in a matter of seconds. On the main road within a minute. He drove with his windows down, letting the night air -with a bit of help from his energy drink to awaken his relaxed senses. He sped along the deserted highway checking the pinpoint location on his GPS screen. Final destination in six minutes' time. Damien gazed up at the crystalline night sky and exhaled. '*No more clouds. Summer is just around the corner*'. He loathed rainy days. Days when he was forced to remain indoors with his German Shepherd and his thoughts. The dog was good company; his mind was not. Memory lane was a horror road for Damien. He shook his head as he made a right turn into the silent village. Old stone houses mingled with a few newer ones revealing that the younger generation had fled to the main town of the island and even toward the city of Athens. One street on the village's outskirts had their lights on. No one stood outside but Damien noticed many eyes peering out from the safety of their homes. He was the first to arrive on the scene. For comfort he turned on his siren lights to let the residents know that help had arrived. He entered through the open gate and drove up the small hill. The enormous mansion now rose before him, blanketed in darkness. He parked away from the building and stepped out of his vehicle, leaving the lights on. Red and blue danced upon the dull grey rocks, illuminating the massive ivy that had conquered most of the wall. Damien fixed his belt and pulled out his gun. He took a few short steps forward. Only silence welcomed him.

'Hello? This is Lieutenant Damien Levante with Corfu Police...'

The sound of the front door being pushed open made him jump. A shadow was coming toward him. The limping figure came into the light provided by his running car's headlights. A young red-haired woman, dressed in only her underwear and covered in blood, came out of the mansion weeping and with her arms stretched out, begging for help.

'Miss, are you hurt? Where have you been hurt, ma'am?' Damien asked as the woman collapsed in front of him. He knelt by her side.

'I was stabbed in the leg,' she struggled to say.

'Who else is in the house?'

Her blue eyes looked straight into his. 'No one. They are all dead.' The woman replied with pain coloring her every word. She closed her eyes as she settled her head upon his leg.

'Miss, try to stay awake. Help is on its way. What's your name?'

She swallowed what felt like a slab blocking her throat. She could taste the blood in her mouth. 'Zoe. I'm the old lady's nurse.'

'Where is the old lady now?'

'Dead! I said, they are all dead! She's dead and she fucking killed my boyfriend! Leo...' Tears fell uncontrollably as Damien called in to check on the arrival of the police unit and to request an ambulance.

'Miss, I have to get my first aid kit from my car. You are bleeding out. We need to apply pressure immediately.'

The woman looked up at her savior, mesmerized by his rich, husky, authoritative voice. She felt drowsy and blamed her fragile state of mind for concentrating on the handsome man's chiselled features and row of symmetrically perfect white teeth. She felt secure near him and that is all that mattered to her at that moment. Anything to not think of all the death that took place inside the mansion.

Two cars arrived simultaneously as Damien was attending to her deep cut, shooting a spasm of pain through her weak body. Two young officers exited the police vehicle, while Damien's partner Anneta jumped out of her car and rushed up to him.

'Stay with her. Help is on the way,' he said looking at the two men in their twenties dressed in their police uniforms. One thing he missed, one he did not. To be young again was a thought of his that occurred often. But just the thought of wearing the navy-blue clothes with the uncomfortable black shoes, made his dinner float upward.

'Let's get inside. The girl said everyone is dead; but who knows?'

Anneta took out her firearm and followed him inside. 'Did she say who the attacker was?'

Damien shook his head. He was already by the door. 'Corfu Police! Anyone here?' He ran his hand against the wall inside and switched on the lights. The vast living room lit up as expensive chandeliers came alive revealing fine furniture, walls featuring art and an enormous fireplace dominating the room. Upon it were dozens of frames of various sizes. Most featured black and white photos, some were of colorful family moments and some sat empty. Damien's eyes looked at the blood stains on the dark brown parquet floor. He followed them to the corridor. The lights were on. A woman's body lay before him. She wore a pair of bloody jeans and a ripped black T-shirt. Her red hair was stuck to her bruised forehead and mingled with the blood oozing out. A massive wound through the chest was responsible for painting her clothes red.

'Dear Lord.' Anneta's voice came from behind him. 'Look.'

In the middle of the long corridor a man's hand lay alone on the carpet, while at the end of the corridor an old lady dressed in a pink nightgown sat apparently dead next to the wall. 'Go check on the old lady. I'll go find the owner of the arm.' Damien stood up and called out once again. Still no reply.

Damien reached a bedroom door. Faint light was provided by an antique lamp on a cherry wood bedside table. The owner of the hand was definitely dead. He lay in a pool of blood in the middle of the king-sized bed. A butcher's knife stuck out of his neck, having made it halfway nearly decapitating him. The man with the now permanent shocked expression was in his late forties and completely naked.

'The old woman is dead,' Anneta called out.

'Hand's owner, too. We have to secure the house. Make sure no one else is here.'

The ambulance siren broke the silence as the two investigators made their way around the mansion, checking it, room by room. Stuffy air welcomed them as much of the enormous house was no longer used. The upper floor had not been used in years. But nothing compared to the putrid smell emanating from the basement. Damien covered his mouth and nose as he kicked in the locked door and the nasty odor escaped. He waited a second before taking a deep breath and descending the cement steps. The decaying body of a headless young man lay on an old, worn-out green sofa. His skin had crawled into itself, and blood had pooled, a victim of gravity, as no beating heart existed to circulate it. Flies attracted by the foul smell buzzed around him and as Damien moved closer, he noticed maggots slithering near the neck wound. Based on the putrefaction, Damien knew the body was at least a month old. '*What the hell went down in this house?*'

Chapter Two

Her eyes fought to open. The intense white light scarred her pupils. Her head felt as heavy as an elephant carrying a whale. She smiled at the thought of her grandma's silly saying. The constant beeping noises around her were growing in volume. Voices echoed around her, but she could not make out clear words.

'She's waking up.'

Yes, that is what the male voice said. She was sure. Her dry lips parted. Her breath came out with difficulty. She was not sure if she had spoken or not. She felt like smiling but resisting. A euphoric feeling spread inside of her.

'Can you hear me? I am Dr. Helena Petra. What is your name?'

'*What is it with everyone asking me my name tonight?*' She raised her hands and stroked her leg. The pain had gone. Her wound was dressed. She felt the need to touch her cross hanging from a thin chain around her neck. 'Zoe,' she managed to say, and the word scratched her throat as it escaped her trembling mouth.

'Zoe, you are going to be just fine, dear. You are a fighter. Very strong. But you need to rest and relax. Let your system take care of itself.'

'*God, she talks a lot for a doctor with such a strict face.*' She fixed her head on the soft pillow. 'Thank you.' She slurred the two words. It reminded her of that one time she felt anything remotely similar to a hangover. A night of gin and wine with old friends from school. She was never much of a drinker.

'Is there anyone we should call? A relative?'

She shook her head. 'No, no. I am not from around here. I came to work as a nurse for an elderly woman and...'

'Surely your parents would like to know that you are alright, even if they live far away.'

Zoe sat up uneasily. She could see the tips of nearby conifers from the lone window of the room. 'I'm an orphan.'

'Oh...' The doctor looked down at her notes. She was not reading. Just avoiding Zoe's gaze. 'If you need anything from us, do not hesitate to call. Just press this button and a nurse will be here for you.'

'Some water would be nice.'

A male nurse who was standing silently to her left came forward and poured her a glass of water from a small bottle on a plastic wheeled bedside table. It was cold. Just as she liked her water to be. Her lips welcomed it with joy.

Another nurse with blonde hair and pretty features popped her head through the door. 'Doctor, there is a detective here for you.'

Doctor Helena stood unimpressed by the man waiting for her by the fake bushes placed in big cheap Japanese-knockoff vases. Damien stood nearby the row of windows that provided precious light to the long hallway during the day. From behind her thin reading glasses, her beady-eyed look fled and headed straight to the scruffy-looking man that introduced himself as a police lieutenant. Helena had a strong sense of smell, and she could tell when smoke, strong deodorant and chewing gum blended to cover up a residual scent of alcohol. She thought of the hour and tried to bring a certain amount of logic to her inner judgement of the man. *'He was probably off duty and had been just called in.'*

'...so, as you can see, it is of the utmost importance that I speak to the witness as soon as possible. Every second and every detail matters...'

Hesitation sparks went off inside her mind but having heard the number of bodies found inside the mansion, she reluctantly agreed that the Lieutenant could visit her patient.

'But at the first sign of distress or agitation, you're out.'

Damien nodded in agreement. 'You've got it, doc. Sure thing.' He fixed his belt as he walked up to the door and ran his long fingers through his hair. He knocked twice and opened the white door. The woman that had run out to him surely looked better. Her cheeks had found their lost rosy color and her eyes seemed more alive. He hoped she had the strength to retell her ordeal. 'May I join you?' he asked, and headed toward the armchair by her bed. 'Feeling better, I presume?'

'They have doped me up pretty well because I am feeling no pain.'

She spoke without struggle. Damien felt confident about his following question. 'Miss Zoe, believe me, the last thing I wish is to bother you at such an hour and under such circumstances, but experience has taught me that our mind tends to lose details even of the strongest memories as the minutes fly by. Would you be brave enough to cope with some questions?'

Zoe swallowed the lump lingering inside her throat. 'What is it you want to know exactly?'

'Everything.'

Zoe closed her eyes. 'Where do I even start?'

He could see her eyes watering up. He could not afford to lose his witness to sentiment. '*Get her to start from happier moments.*' He forced a smile. 'How about you tell me where you are from and about the day you found the job as the old lady's nurse?'

Zoe scratched her forehead and exhaled. 'It was only a week ago and yet it seems so far away. So much has happened since I arrived on the island.'

Damien looked up at her. He had been preparing his notepad and his blue pen. 'Not from Corfu?'

'I came from Ioannina.'

Damien leaned forward. 'How did you find the job? Answered an ad?'

'No, no. I had just finished nursing school and I needed a job. I did not want to work in a hospital.' She paused and laughed. 'Tragic but I hate these places because of too much death. Oh, the irony. So, I signed up with an agency offering my services as a live-in nurse. You see, I was raised by nuns in the orphanage in Ioannina and I needed a place to live. The agency covered Epirus, West Greece and all the Ionian Islands. I told them I preferred an island. I needed to get away from the rain and the snow. I am an islander in my heart. I need the sun and the sea. And I have one lone passion in life, diving.'

'*She's a talker. Good.*'

'So, the agency set you up? What agency is this?'

'*Nurses, SOS.* They said they had a wealthy client that

needed a young girl to live with her. I spoke on the phone with her daughter in Athens and she made all the arrangements.'

'What's the daughter's name, and do you still have her number?'

Zoe looked out of the window and wiped her eyes. 'Her name was Alice. She is one of the bodies in the house.'

'Who killed them? We are on an island. If your attacker is on the run, we need to get the coast guard...'

Zoe raised her palm. 'No one to chase, detective. We are all killers. It was a fight till the death. I was the only one who managed to get out.'

'And what about the basement?' He left out the description. 'Anyone go down there last night?'

Zoe's eyes opened wide, and her entire body twitched. 'I have no idea, Lieutenant. It was always locked without a key in sight. What was in the...?' She exhaled as she shook her head. 'Detective, I am clueless about the basement. Never been down there. I have only been living there for the past few days before...' She swallowed another lump in her throat. She looked around for water. A small glass stood on her bedside cabinet. Damien brought it closer to her and as she drank, he said, 'I think you're going to have to tell me your whole story as to get to the bottom of this.'

Chapter Three

3 days ago

Zoe sat close to the slightly opened car window. Near enough to avoid choking on the heavy cologne dominating the confined space of the vehicle. It rose off the sweaty taxi driver who wore a checkered shirt that was missing a button. Yet not near enough as to inhale any part of the cloud of dust that the speeding car had given birth to as it sped down these country roads. She held on to the grab handle as the driver attacked the road's speed-control bumps. She regretted entering the maniac's taxi, but it was too late now for regrets. After stepping off the boat from the mainland, her stomach was a swimming pool on a stormy windy night, she was too dizzy to be fussy. She had approached the first driver she laid eyes upon. She had wobbled across the street, dressed in her light-blue dress -a gift from the nuns for her degree ceremony, rolling her luggage behind her and had walked up to the tall man with the long black beard and the heavy gold cross semi-lost in the thickness of his chest hair.

'Saint John's village? Livos Mansion at the end of Anexartisias Street?' Her voice had been reserved and low.

'Huh? Speak up, girl.'

Zoe had repeated her desired destination and watched as the large man picked up her suitcase, threw it in the back, opened a door for her and squeezed into his car. He had then switched on the radio and stepped on the gas. Zoe found the music deafening but then again it meant there was no talking from the driver. Greek taxi drivers were notorious talkers and believed themselves experts on every topic, ranging from politics to sports.

The vehicle coming to a halt made her reopen her eyes. She had closed them and tried to get lost in prayer.

'Here, little missy. Gates are closed. You calling them or walking in?'

'Walk. Walking. Yes,' she replied, and her black shoes touched the gravelled road as she practically dove outside. It felt good to be safe on solid ground again.

There was a side door to the main gate, and it swung happily, creaking in the wind that reigned permanently on the hill. Zoe formed the sign of the cross on her chest. Then she took a deep breath and began her walk up to the hilltop villa. An aroma settled on the entrance of her nostrils. A blend of roses and citrus flowers. Zoe took a moment to look around. The gardens were perfectly kept, in full contrast to the walls of the house that stood defeated by time and the weather. Zoe was not sure for how long she remained outside the main door, contemplating knocking or ringing. She could not delay the inevitable any longer. She had to dive into the deep end. Her first job. Her new home. Her first home, really.

Her index finger pushed the white button and a ring

echoed around inside the house. 'The key is under the cactus pot,' an old lady's voice came from a window further down. 'Okay, ma'am.' Zoe looked down at the three cactus pots ganged up in the corner of the bricked wall. She found the key on her first go and smiled at the fact. *'Good luck all the way, I hope.'*

In and around went the key and the door to her new life opened. Zoe gawked at the wealth spread out before her. She had never witnessed such a living room before. Ample light journeyed in from the row of open windows, their draperies prancing upon the breeze.

'Hurry up, girl. Don't keep me waiting.' The harsh voice travelled toward her, giving haste to her tired feet. The corridor smelled of detergent. Wild berries. Everything was spotless. Zoe could not believe that she was going to be living in such extravagant surroundings. The first door revealed an empty bedroom, so she quickly dashed for the next. A large bed conquered much of the space. The curtains were thick and drawn shut. The only light came from an old lamp that was placed on the floor even though two empty bedside tables existed on either side of the antique bed. Zoe remained in the doorway looking at the shadowy figure sitting up on the bed, supported by a number of white pillows. 'Switch on the lights, girl, let me get a better look at you!'

'Shall I open the curtains, ma'am?' Zoe asked, thinking of the strong, beautiful sunlight that filled up the rest of the house.

'Did I say such a thing? Learn to listen. Lesson one. Do as I say.'

Zoe's shaking hand pulled the switch down and the chandelier brought light to the room. Both women gazed at each other. Zoe with her head still and a genuine smile on her flushed face, saw her new boss.

She was definitely not like the old ladies at the orphanage that Zoe was used to.

No benign expression was to be found.

A still face bordering on angry was hidden among messy gunmetal-grey hair. Her thin lips formed a straight line and small honey-colored eyes rested in the centre of deep crow's feet. A slightly crooked nose reminded Zoe of evil Disney witches and the time-ravaged yellowy skin did not help matters. A gold chain hung from her neck featuring a cross and a small key that fell into a gang of pea-sized moles. Zoe lowered her gaze. She did not wish to be seen shocked by the sickly appearance of her new boss/patient. The old lady's hands were inflamed, and her nails were begging for a good cut.

'Why are you just standing there like an idiot, child? Come closer. Hand me my glasses so I can also study you.'

'Yes, ma'am.'

'The name is Mirela. Cut the ma'am crap. Times have changed, you know.'

Mirela's hand trembled as she struggled to wear the black thick-framed glasses just handed to her. 'Hmmm, you sure is a pretty one, child. Clean face, slim figure, rich hair. I hope we don't have men knocking on my door at all hours.'

'Of course not, ma'...Mrs. Mirela. Definitely not. I am here for you and to help you get better.'

'No one gets better after a lifetime of illness. I'm too weak to fight any longer. You cannot turn back the hands of treacherous time. I doubt I have many years left in me.' Mirela's voice broke. Zoe wondered if her gravel voice was due to a dry throat. She poured the old lady a glass of water from the bottle on the bed stand. 'Here you go. Yes, we cannot beat time, but we can surely make our final years much more comfortable. And that is why I am here. I will truly work for your health and convenience.'

Mirela sniggered. 'Is that a poem you learnt at nursing school? Do you really believe that, child?'

'I wouldn't be here if I didn't!'

Mirela closed her eyes and shook her head. 'Your optimism is annoying. Go see your room.' She waved her hand. 'It's two doors down, to your right. Relax from your journey. Then go get familiarized with the kitchen. Lunch time is approaching.'

Zoe smiled and retreated without speaking. She picked up her luggage that she had left in the long corridor and headed to her allocated quarters. Her room was smaller than Mirela's but much brighter. Both windows were open and ample light and fresh air filled the room with the single bed and the empty bedside table. Zoe closed the door behind her, sat down on the soft mattress and exhaled loudly with a sigh. She took her phone into her hand. She felt the need to hear Leo's voice.

'No, Zoe. Resist.'

She left the cell on the bed and approached the window. 'Talk to yourself.' She gazed out and admired the unobstructed view of beautiful blossoming meadows that ran up to the first stone village houses. *'What have I gotten myself into? She is going to be difficult to work with. Strong-willed and bossy. Weird how her daughter described her as bedridden with Alzheimer's. Who takes care of the house? Who opened my windows? Who cooked yesterday? Probably a lady from the village.'* Zoe looked back into the room. 'A room of my own.' Zoe walked slowly around the bed, her hand running along its cherry wood. She let the thought sink in. She could not remember a time when she had her own room. There were always at least three girls sharing a room at the monastery's orphanage. During her studies she stayed with two other girls with limited funds on campus for the first two years and then with another orphan roommate at a nun-owned apartment for the rest of her nursing course. She smiled with the thought and opened the wardrobe doors. One side was completely vacant, obviously emptied for her. The other side was overrun by cupboard boxes of various sizes, all taped shut and squeezed into place. Whistling to her latest favorite tune, Zoe unpacked and neatly tidied her few belongings away. After one more look outside at the serene image painted by nature, and taking a deep breath, Zoe exited her room and as her lady commanded, she headed to the kitchen at the end of the hall. The neglected, dusty blinds were lowered all the way and the room was dark. Zoe did not switch on the light as she always opted for sunlight. More natural, more alive, warmer. Sunrays invaded as the worn blinds rose and Zoe gazed around her. It was a kitchen from an era long gone. A country kitchen from the fifties, yet the electrical appliances gave the correct century away. The fridge and cupboards were well stocked. *'I have to impress.'* Zoe looked at the clock hanging on the brick wall to her left. She had plenty of time. She placed the salmon on the wooden counter and left it to defrost while she gathered the rest of the ingredients that she had in mind.

Zoe contemplated turning on the radio but decided not to risk it. Music was her companion. Through thick and thin, music helped her escape. Escape her true life, her thoughts, her depression. The house was quiet, too quiet. *'Has she fallen asleep? What does she do all day? Both her kids are away...'* Zoe walked silently with light feet towards Mirela's door. She stood behind the closed door and brought her right ear to its cool surface.

'What is it, child? Why are you lingering outside my door?'

Zoe jumped back, quickly collected herself and opened the door.

'Did I say you could enter?'

'I'm sorry, ma'am... Mrs. Mirela.'

Mirela rolled her eyes in dramatic fashion making sure Zoe saw her. 'Well, you're here now. Pour me some water.'

Zoe approached. 'Time for your pink pills, too.'

'All I do is take pills. A rainbow of them from dawn to dusk. I'm fed up, child. This is not living.'

Zoe passed her the two pills and a glass of water. 'Don't talk like that,' she said with a genuine smile, sparkling eyes and an upbeat tone. 'Life is what we make of it. What is it that you enjoy doing most? Maybe its time for a new hobby.'

Mirela's notorious sniggering followed. 'You really are an optimistic fool.'

'Better than a pessimistic Einstein.'

Mirela's croaky laughter echoed around the room. A laughter that raised her chest and brought on a terrible cough. 'Your humor will kill me, girl. You are a funny one.'

Suddenly, Mirela's face went cold. She closed her eyes and pointed to her right. 'There's someone at the door.'

Zoe looked at her patient. Her mouth opened but she was unsure on what to say. She just stroked the old lady's wrinkly hand and got up to leave. Just then, the doorbell rang. With the sound of the bell, Mirela lowered her hand. Zoe licked her lips and rushed out of the room to answer the door. Another ring followed. 'I'm coming,' she called out. Her right hand grabbed the golden door handle, and she pulled the heavy door toward her. No one was there. Zoe stepped outside and gazed around. 'Hello?' The day breeze had lost its cool as the ferocious Greek sun made its ascent to the clear blue sky above. Zoe felt like a Lady from one of her medieval romance novels, exiting her castle upon the hill and laying her eyes on the village below as the commoners went about with their daily duties. The front garden was mostly empty. A twisty olive tree stood at her right while now she noticed a row of neglected rose bushes that ran along the side path leading up to the porch. All around was yellowy grass begging for salvation, for water, for its long-lost green days. 'Is there anyone there?' she asked as she walked around the mansion remembering that she was not there to inspect and judge the yard. 'Probably kids annoying the old lady. Pranksters!' She shook her head. 'She heard them outside. That is how she knew.'

Zoe returned inside and decided to go straight to the kitchen. She had lunch to prepare. Besides, the TV blared loudly from Mirela's room. She was not needed, nor did she have to explain who was not at the door.

At half past noon exactly, Zoe entered her patient's room with a full tray in hand.

'Lunch is ready,' she announced as she closed the door behind her with her body. The salmon smelled divine, cooked in virgin olive oil and fresh lemons. Asparagus, broccoli, and carrots gave the dish color. A tall glass of lemonade filled with ice cubes crackling at its top, a small plate with a square piece of milk chocolate and an array of pills in a see-through plastic cup made up the gang occupying the silver serving tray. The glow on Zoe's face revealed how proud she was of her presentation. A short-lived glow as Mirela looked startled.

'What? Who are you? What the hell are you doing in my house? Where is my daughter? Alice? Alice? Help!' Mirela raised her voice with each word until her cough strangled her words and silenced her. Zoe quickly placed the salver on the bedside table and rushed to her patient's aid.

'Relax, Mrs. Mirela. It's me. Zoe. Your nurse. Zoe.' She repeated her name, hoping for a memory jolt. She stroked the old woman's hand and smiled widely. Mirela's eyes trembled and watered up. 'My nurse?'

Zoe shook her head. 'I am here to take care of you. I am Zoe. You have nothing to fear. Everything will go just fine. I have cooked your favorite. Salmon. Alice, your daughter, sent me a list of foods you enjoy.'

Mirela's heavy breathing relaxed. 'Where is that ungrateful bitch? Her mother is in pain, prisoned upon a damn bed. Where is she? Partying with men and drinking and dancing…'

'She is in Athens, Mrs. She is a… businesswoman.' Zoe was not exactly sure what her profession was. 'I am sure she would love to be here with you, but people must work. She loves you very much and cares as much as to hire me to…'

Mirela closed her eyes and turned away. 'Just feed me and be quiet, child. You know nothing. Lesson two. Keep your opinions to your bloody self.'

All forty-eight spoonfuls were served in silence. The pills followed, helped down by a gulp of lemonade. The chocolate was there to remove the nasty after taste of the drug cocktail. 'Now quickly leave. I need to take a shit. Come back in twenty minutes to change me. Out!'

Zoe obeyed in silence. *'What a vulgar, bitter old witch!'* she thought on her way to the kitchen to clean up. *'I hope I never end up as lonely and angry as she.'*

Zoe went about with her chores and duties for the rest of the day without speaking much. To Mrs. Mirela that was as she drove herself halfway to crazy with all her inner chatter. Nightfall came as a relief. Her ankles ached -too much

23

for a twenty-three-year-old woman. '*Must be the long journey here.*' Her eyes felt heavy. She saw them staring back at her in the hallway mirror. Red and puffy. The expensive antique did not lie.

'Goodnight, Mrs. Mirela,' she wished as she gave her the last pills of the day. The old woman swallowed them without water, grunted and turned to her side. Zoe switched off the lights and gladly returned to her room for a much-needed shower. Zoe had never seen an en-suite before. 'All mine.' She showered without rush, enjoying the hot running water and essence shower gel. A young soul deprived of any sort of luxury in life, Zoe often dreamt of a life where she was not an orphan but the daughter of a wealthy family. She dreamt of island breaks and visits to the hair salon. Dining in fine restaurants and wearing designer clothes. 'Reality is a harsh bitch.'

Zoe dressed in the bathroom, a habit of a child growing up with communal spaces. Underwear and a white gown that fell all the way to her knees, covered her body as she stepped back into the room. Her eyes sparkled at the large bed that was waiting for her. She leapt on it and fell back into the soft pillows. She exhaled and released her anxiousness of the first day. 'One down, a thousand to go,' she joked. 'If the old bat lives that much.' Her jaw clenched at the sight of 'no new messages' on her phone. Her ego needed contact from Leo. She wished him to be the first to cave in and reach out. She missed him. His green eyes, his dimples, the warmth of his naked body. He was her first lover and so far, her only.

Zoe was glad that the light switch was just above the bed. She raised her arm and off the light went. Darkness settled and only green screen light shone upon her from her phone as she scrolled through social media looking at her favorite influencers and stars. Their bags, their jewels, their boots, their happiness.

Her morning bus journey out of town, her ferry ride from the port, the taxi to the village and a day of work ganged up and a ton of exhaustion spread on her body. She lowered her phone and as its screen went dark, Zoe noticed the thin line of light below her door.

'*Didn't I turn off the corridor light?*'

Zoe remained in bed. She had just gotten comfortable; her head having created that ideal positional dent in her pillow. '*What if the old lady wakes up before me and shouts about the electrical bill? Nah, with her strong meds, she wakes up after the sun, surely. She will see no light.*' Zoe persuaded herself to stay in bed. Just as her eyes closed, she heard a faint noise coming from the hallway. Her eyes reopened. She focused her attention. Did she hear right? Footsteps? Her heartbeats raced into the hundreds, and she quickly sat up in bed. And there it was, a shadow cutting the slim line of light in half. Someone was standing outside her door. Zoe never imagined herself as the type to freeze. A woman of action, she disappointed herself with her inaction. '*Could it be one of her children?*' Cold sweat formed on the back of her neck and below her hairline on her forehead. A new terrifying thought. '*A thief. A rapist. A murderer.*' She finally got her feet to obey, and she crept up to the door and as quietly as possible she turned the key. The locked door offered her a sense of security. She let out a soundless sigh. She placed her ear on the door and waited. Nothing. Silence had returned to the house.

'Michael? Michael?'

Mirela's calls grew louder.

'*Who the hell is Michael? Great. The old lady now thinks the burglar is someone she knows.*' Zoe walked over to her nightstand and picked up her phone. 'I'm calling the police.' She whispered the words, but her fingers never moved. '*And if it was a trick of the light? A shadow from outside? My sleepy eyes playing tricks? I am not going to embarrass myself on my first day…*'

Zoe had a talent for driving herself crazy in thought.

'Michael? Michael?' Where are you, my boy?'

'*Could she have a dog and forgotten about it? The daughter did not say such a thing, but she never visits much…*'

Zoe's tongue ran along her dried lip. A sign of deep thought, of coming up with a plan. She wore her white trainers and opened the window. The air outside was clean and cool. '*What's the point of air conditioning?*' With the power of her youth, she jumped and landed with ease on the dying grass. She tiptoed up to Mirela's window. It was open just an inch for fresh air. Zoe slid the window aside and climbed in. Faint light was provided by a single lamp placed on the floor in the corner of the room next to a porcelain pot featuring a shrub too green to be real. Thankfully, the old lady's bed faced away from the window. She was still mumbling the same name.

'Mrs. Mirela? It's Zoe. Your nurse. I am here. What's wrong, ma'am?'

'My son. My son, Michael came to visit. Where is he?'

'Your son is Theodore. He is off studying, remember? Mrs. Mirela, do you own a dog?'

The old lady quit her tossing and turning and looked straight at her with an icy gaze. 'What are you on about, you damn fool? Michael is my youngest. He is here. No, I don't have no bloody dog. They smell and shit all over the place and need attention. Go out and look around. See who is here.'

Zoe's facial and neck muscles clenched. 'I… I am scared.'

26

Mirela's sinister laugh made her skin crawl. 'The little orphan is scared of the night! How much worse can happen to you, child?'

Zoe held back tears gathering below her trembling eyes. She closed Mirela's window, tucked the old lady in, wished her a good night and exited her room. *'I'd rather be out here with the burglar than with that evil witch.'* The corridor was empty. Zoe headed straight into the kitchen and opened the top drawer. She picked up the biggest knife and began switching on every light. Room by room she checked the massive mansion. Locked and empty. The cellar door was locked with no key in sight; the only room she could not enter. She knelt and looked through the keyhole, flashing her mobile light through it. It appeared deserted. Zoe went upstairs to the closed-off upper floor. When Mirela could no longer use stairs, her bed was brought downstairs.

Zoe kept the knife by her side that night. And just before finally managing to close her eyes, she picked up her phone and sent a text over Messenger. 'Leo, I wish you were here. It is one of those nights. I need you. When can you visit? Good night, x.'

Chapter Four

'Sounds like an awful first night.' Damien spoke as Zoe had stopped retelling her first day and turned for water. She shivered as she tried to reach the water bottle. 'Here, let me.' Damien walked over and poured her a glass. The woman looked tired and pale. 'Shall we continue?'

Zoe pulled down the white sheet that was covering her body. She wore only a hospital gown and multiple stitches on her right thigh. Her eyes focused on the wound. It seemed smaller than she expected. When the knife slid through her, she thought she would lose her leg. The excruciating pain was like no other. She remembered the amount of blood that oozed out of her. And now, all it caused her was a mania to scratch. An itchy long red line upon her leg, taunting her. Taunting her about all the different choices she could have made and changed the deadly outcome. But what was done, was done and the detective was waiting. Yet, the Lieutenant had walked over to the window and was staring outside. That is when Zoe realized how see-through the cheap, thin gown was. She had made him feel uncomfortable. She pulled up the sheet and wiggled to get back into a cosy position. 'I need some sleep, officer. I promise I won't forget anything. How could I? This will loiter in my nightmares until my final breath. It will be morning soon and the light and the nurses will invade my room in a couple of hours.'

Damien scratched his right eyebrow and continued down to his unshaved cheek. 'Yeah, yeah. You're probably right,' he agreed in a reluctant tone. 'I'll be back in a few hours then.'

Zoe's eyes seemed to be sparkling. They had watered up. Damien wondered if the meds were wearing off or if the pain was from the memories of the night. 'Please, turn off the light. It's burning my eyes. I've been awake for twenty-two hours straight.'

'Sure thing, Miss Zoe. Have a much-needed rest. We will talk in the morning.'

Damien's two-bedroom apartment was not far from Corfu's main hospital. He chose it as it was one of the only blocks that provided underground parking. A luxury in the small town where there seemed to be more cars than humans, if possible. Wherever you went, it was a struggle to find where to park. Now, the gate opened, and his allocated spot was there waiting for him. It was the only one that was empty. No other tenants out at four in the morning. For Damien, it was the norm.

At least this time he was not stumbling in, drunk into nirvana, intoxicated into an oblivion of thoughtless heaven.

He always returned alone. Any time he *got lucky*; a cheap hotel owner *got lucky* as well.

The only female his home needed woke up as he closed the door behind him.

'Hey, Jolie,' he said as the canine rushed towards him, her nails scraping along the white tiles. He knelt and let the German Shepherd lick his cheek as her tail whipped the floor. 'Who's a good girl? Huh? Who's the best? You are. Yes, you are,' he said in the same tone most used on babies. His fingers ran through her thick coat and white and brown hairs scattered around them. 'Not built for a Greek island, are you dear? Too hot, who's too hot?' He stood up and looked over at her two bowls. Both were half empty. Her water and food were probably the only things in his daily routine that he worried about. He filled up her water, stroked her head and stepped on the envelopes that had been thrown under his door as his mailbox below had been overpowered by supermarket and kebab shop flyers. 'Final notice!' He mocked the words. 'I will pay you Mr. Electricity. I think I haven't gambled away all my wage yet.' Jolie wiggled around him as he continued speaking in the tone that he only used with her. Damien sighed, kicked the envelopes to the side and headed into the kitchen. The light scared a rather large cockroach that was standing on top of his leftover microwave mac and cheese with chunks of chicken. Damien did not care enough to chase it. The air was stale, carrying an odor of fried eggs and milk gone bad. Damien opened the window an inch and ordered the night breeze to cleanse the room. He then grabbed a packet of paprika-flavored chips from the cupboard on his left and kicking off his shoes, he trotted to his bedroom. He undressed to his underwear and rubbed his lower back.

That is when he noticed. His bedside table was empty. 'Where is...?' He did not manage to finish his sentence and his eye caught a glimpse of the Jack Daniels bottle that lay on the floor by the bed. Jack was a good whiskey for its price, but it was not his top choice.

He chose it for home due to its shape. Round bottles rolled away from him, hiding under the bed or among tossed clothes. Or worse, travelled too far than he could manage to walk. Jack with its square shape stayed where it fell. He raised the bottle and shook it, smiling at the half-full whiskey bottle. He took off the cap and brought it to his lips. He devoured his morning snack in a matter of minutes, sharing with Jolie who had jumped upon the bed and settled by his leg. He washed the chips down with the rest of the whiskey, set his alarm clock to go off in two hours and eleven minutes, and with a heavy head, he closed his eyes.

He could have sworn only five seconds had passed since he drifted off and the beeping sound echoing from his phone woke him. At least it saved him from the same dream. His nemesis. The repeating nightmare.

Jolie did not move a muscle as he threw off his boxer shorts, sat on the toilet playing Fruit Ninja on his phone, took a two-minute shower, dressed, made a frappe, served her beef from a tin, and exited the front door with a lit Assos cigarette stuck to his bottom lip. 'In my next life, I'm coming back as a dog. Or a cat born at a grandma's house.'

Last in, first out. All cars were still resting; his was the first to break the silence underground. He came up to the quiet street and squinted his eyes at the strong morning rays that welcomed him. He threw on his shades and turned left. Besides the bakery and the corner cafe, all shops were still closed. Few people, mostly elderly, wandered around at such an early hour. Soon, chaos, honking and swearing, would erupt. The straight line to the hospital took seven minutes while the scenic route by the sea took thirteen. Damien lit his second cigarette for the day and opted for a blue background than one of grey, dull buildings and weeds growing high in the sunburnt earth. The Ionian did not disappoint. It never did. A magnificent carpet of clear waters all the way to the horizon, sparkling as the sunrays danced upon the tips of short-lived waves. Some dying upon sandy beaches, some upon austere scintillating rocks. The seagulls provided the lyrics to the music of the sea. Damien drove with his window down and his radio off. You never got any decent songs anyway at such an hour. Just mellow tunes interrupted by snippets of depressing news. At least, that was his conviction.

He arrived at his destination, finished off his coffee and lit a third cigarette as he walked up to the main entrance, shaking off bad memories from the depressing hospital. He stood by the side, near a climbing ivy until he smoked it all down to its bud.

'Hard to quit, huh? Maybe you should switch to vaping,' a lanky nurse said as he exhaled a large cloud of smoke. It smelled like forest fruit. Damien stepped on his dying bud, and without eye contact, said, 'I guess you're a vegan and always politically correct, too, huh? Vices are meant to harm you. If you like wild berries and strawberries, just buy yourself a fucking croissant, muppet.'

A bunch of sickly-looking people and worried relatives waited for the elevator. Damien opted for the stairs. '*And the captain says I never work out.*' His mind journeyed to the pretty girl with the stabbed leg. The image of her wobbly teary eyes as she tried to run towards him replayed in his mind. '*Poor thing.*' As he pushed back the heavy fire exit door, he wondered if she had gained his sympathy due to her looks and how she reminded him of *her*.

Outside of Zoe's room, a short male doctor was asking two nurses in spotless white robes about his patient. '...she woke up a bit disoriented. We told her specifics about her leg and condition, and she just lay there staring at us.'

'She did smile though,' the other one, the older one, commented. 'She seems sad. She's only a child really. Twenty-something and to live through such an ordeal.'

'She seems older, though...'

'Ladies, concentrate,' the doctor said and chuckled. He knew his staff well. They always gossiped and even though he never admitted it, he rather enjoyed it.

Damien walked over and introduced himself. The morning doctor was far more welcoming than the one from the night shift. In her defense though, Damien did realize he was well more presentable at that moment. The black circles below his reddish eyes could be seen as a sign of an overworked public servant and smelling of cheap cigarettes compared to cheap booze, made a huge difference.

'She is doing just fine. That one is a fighter. She may not seem it, but she has a strong spirit. The wound will heal, leaving just a thin scar behind.'

'All wounds leave us with scars. Depends how much we let them get to us.'

The doctor was not expecting a philosophical reply. He nodded his head. 'Yes, yes, of course,' he said and walked off to check up on his next patient. A boy with a broken arm, a worried mum, and an angry dad. The expensive brand-new bike was totally wrecked.

Damien knocked and entered the room, wishing Zoe a good morning. The nurse had just finished drinking a glass of milk. Zoe quickly wiped her white lips with her right hand and sat up straight. 'Good morning, Lieutenant.' She waited for him to turn and pull near a chair, before running her fingers through her messy hair, hoping the hairs would comply and form a semi-decent style. '*Vanity*,' her inner voice told her off.

'You sure you don't need more sleep? I could return later?' Damien wished for no such thing. He needed her statement as soon as possible. His itch to investigate was growing. He wanted to go up to the house with his partner, talk to the forensics team, go down to the morgue, and sit in on the autopsies. But he had a survivor. Just one. Why gather disperse pieces of a puzzle when the woman before him had the box with the image on it?

'Don't you?'

'Sleep and I have never been friends.'

'I can only sleep in complete darkness and silence.' She raised her hands as to present the environment. Strong sunlight rode in from the window overseeing the East and above them four powerful fluorescent lights were switched on. Voices and footsteps made up the commotion outside her doors that had a gap between them, allowing every single sound to journey through.

'If my mind offers me silence, then I sleep.'

'And if it doesn't?'

'I silence it.'

Zoe chuckled but controlled her laughter as she noticed that the Lieutenant was not joking. She wanted to ask how, but knew the question was far too intrusive. There was something about the man though that stirred her pot of curiosity. She kept trying to order herself to behave, to remind herself that she had just lived through a massacre, saw dead bodies for the first time in her life, yet her mind blurred the blood and focused on the officer with the badly ironed clothes sitting by her bed.

'Shall we pick up where we left of? After your first night?'

'Eager to purge my memory, detective? Do not fear. I have forgotten nothing. Every single detail has been burnt into my brain.'

Chapter Five

Zoe's alarm clock went off just before sunrise. Mirela's daughter had mentioned that her mother enjoyed a good sleep, but Zoe wanted to be awake whenever her boss called out to her. She also wanted to familiarize herself with the cookbook that the daughter had left for her on the kitchen counter. The dishes were mainly from the Greek cuisine which was a relief. The young woman had never left Greece before nor had dined in more restaurants than fingers on a hand.

The house remained silent even after she enjoyed a cup of tea and two slices of toast overflowing with honey. Zoe decided to check the medical cabinet. She held the piece of paper with her notes and prepared the day's pills. Her daughter was not good with the various names and had given her instructions by pill color over the phone. Zoe looked down at her scribblings. 'Two pink and white ones... one dark green...'

Having prepared three colorful sets in small white cups for the day (after breakfast, after lunch and after dinner),

Zoe looked up at the clock. Half past eight. All the old ladies she knew woke up with the sun. She began to worry. *'Imagine her dying the first night that I was here. I would never find work again.'* Then again, the only other senior women that Zoe knew were nuns and the landlady she had had during her studies, who was a baker. Not really a perfect demographic as to come to any logical conclusions about age and hour of awaking from slumber.

Still she walked up to Mirela's door, knelt, and peeked through the keyhole. Zoe placed her hand over her mouth and swallowed a gasp as she fell back. Mirela was sitting up, eyes and mouth wide open, with her arms stretched out towards the door.

'Michael? Is that you?'

Zoe stood up, dusted herself off even though the house was spotless, and rushed into the room. 'Good morning, Mrs. Mirela. It is me. Zoe. Your nurse.'

Mirela fell back into her pillows disappointed. 'Change my piss and then go get my pills and breakfast. Be quick about it.'

Zoe nodded, obeyed, and then left the room without speaking. She returned with a tray consisting of eggs, toast, jams, and coffee. Of course, the pills accompanied the delicious meal. Zoe helped her eat and then took her blood pressure and temperature.

'Someone's at the door.' Mirela rolled her eyes upwards, making her pupils disappear. Zoe felt a shiver run down her back. Tiny hairs stood at attention on her neck. She turned towards the bedroom's door. No one was there. Just then, the sound of the doorbell echoed through the house.

'How did you know?'

'Michael loves pranks.'

Zoe swallowed the lump in her throat and slowly walked

out of the room and headed to the front door. Another ring. She ran for the door and opened it with a fast pull. No one was there. She dashed outside and looked around. 'Hello?'

Zoe walked all around the house. No one was to be seen. She looked down at the village. The first houses were a two-minute run away. She returned to the house, trying to control her breathing. 'Breathe in through the nose, exhale from the mouth.' She remembered her P.E. coach's advice when out of breath and with an accelerated heartbeat. As she entered the room, with a dozen questions hanging on the tip of her tongue, the old lady spoke loudly. 'I want a bath today. This isn't the civil war when we washed just once a week.'

'Of course,' Zoe replied. 'A sponge bath in bed or do you wish to lay in the tub?'

'Tub.'

It is a delicate moment for any patient. You feel vulnerable as medical staff carries you, undresses you, sees you naked and then touches your body as to wash it. You feel inadequate, helpless, redundant even. Zoe knew all this. She tried to make the experience less intrusive, less procedural. She played hits from Yianni Pario on her phone (she guessed he was one of Mirela's favorite singers as she had a signed photo autograph from him in a pearly frame in the kitchen), she lit a papaya-scented candle and drew the bathroom curtain half-way as to dim the light.

She also tried to engage the elderly woman in conversation.

Nothing sparked any interest. The weather, the village, her mansion, politics, gossip, TV. Not a single topic received more than a couple of sentences reply.

'Obviously, it's going to be bloody hot, it's summer!'

'Obviously,' Zoe echoed.

'Who cares about the villagers? Do they care about me?'

'Innocent politicians is an oxymoron. Like a virgin whore!'

'Morning TV is for the weak minded!'

Mrs. Mirela had a reply to shut down her every attempt at a decent conversation.

Zoe continued in silence, gently rubbing the woman's back with her sea sponge and letting her nostrils welcome the ethereal aromas from the oils she had put into the hot water. She bit her lower lip and decided to ask.

'Mrs. Mirela, who is Michael?' Zoe squinted her eyes as to prepare for the impact. But Mirela answered calmly. Sweetly even. 'My precious boy. A mother doesn't always admit it, but their youngest ones are usually their favorite ones.'

Zoe contemplated reminding her that her son's name was Theodore but held back. She felt a story brewing. She decided to play along. She placed a lump of citrus-scented shampoo on Mirela's tangled hair and began to massage the old woman's head gently. 'So, Michael is your youngest? Alice is your first and Theodore the second?'

'Was my youngest.'

The way she pronounced the word *was* made Zoe's heart skip a beat. The thought had never crossed her mind.

'I had children late in life. I know you see me as an old woman. I am not. I am only sixty-four years old. Others my age are out and about in cafes and cruising the islands and having affairs. Sixty is the new forty and all that. I know I look near eighty.'

Zoe's expression changed. Saddened. It welcomed a wave of sorrow. Guilt came over her about all her thoughts. She was a fool. The woman had a son attending university.

She should have worked out the maths before labelling her employer as an old lady.

'Don't feel bad. You saw me as I was and thought me an old centenarian bat with one foot in the grave.'

Zoe sat behind Mirela. She looked across and realized her face was visible in the oval mirror above the sink. Zoe began to mouth an 'I'm sorry', but Mirela continued. 'Illnesses have always tried to get the best of me. One virus after another, I beat them all. They left taking a piece of me, but I remained strong. Remained alive. I spent more time on a bed of pain, than living outside. Imagine living in the most beautiful country in the world and being locked up in your room or in a hospital for half of it. This is why, you see, I was late marrying. I met Gianni when I was thirty-eight. He was a builder. He came with a crew to mend and paint some hospital wall during one of my many stays there. His love gave me strength. Me! Sickly Mirela went out! Dating and all! We were married within a year. And despite my weak system and my age, I had my daughter at forty. After treatment, I had Theodore at forty-three and my Michael at forty-four. One big happy family.'

The last sentence did not carry the happy spark the rest had enjoyed. Mirela returned to her usual bitter and harsh tone. She stopped talking. Zoe could not handle the silence. She was dying to know. She dared to ask. 'What happened to Gianni, Mrs. Mirela?'

'That God-damn lovable fool. We took out a loan and bought a small cabin to house our family in his village, Kastoria. As a builder, he swore he was going to fix up the wreck.' Mirela closed her eyes and lay back upon Zoe's hands. 'And then one night, I was really bad. Puking and coughing. He rushed out to go to the chemist. Michael was two at the time and restless. The others were asleep. Gianni took him with him as his old truck always shook little Mickey to sleep. I never saw them again. Some fucking teens, drunk out of their minds, lurched out in front of them. Gianni crushed into them at full speed. Four dead... instantly... for some bloody cough medicine for me! My health went further downhill since then. I prayed to the Lord to take me, but He seems to like watching me suffer.' Mirela groaned to clear her throat. Her last sentences came out as an undertone, a whisper. 'I don't pray anymore. I now know better.'

'Sometimes having faith is all that will get us through.'

Mirela sniggered and waved her right hand as if presenting an award winner. Water splashed around her, foaming up. 'The orphan philosopher, ladies and gentlemen. Oh, child. How clueless you truly are! There are no magical beings to save you from your miserable existence.' Mirela released a sinister laugh. 'And even if there were up there, what good have they ever done to you or me as to deserve any praise?'

Zoe washed out the soap from Mirela's hair and picked up the hairbrush with the silver handle. 'You found love in your life, and you have this fine home...'

'Love?'

'Gianni?'

'Who?' Mirela's gaze had lost its focus. Her eyes moved rapidly around the room. Zoe decided on not reminding her of a dead spouse. 'Time to get up, Mrs. All done. You have such beautiful hair.'

'Yes, it will rot beautifully when I am six feet under.'

Zoe shook her head and realized that no wave of sweetness could extinguish such a raving fire of bitterness.

With Mirela firmly placed back in bed, with milk and cookies by her side, the TV playing and a few magazines by her pillow, Zoe found herself with time to explore the mansion.

Her fingertips ran along expensive vases, Swarovski animal ornaments and exquisite art locked by hand-carved frames. Zoe stood opposite the fireplace and wondered how it would feel like to watch the rising dancing flames, welcome the warmth, and let it caress your body. It was always so cold at the nuns' orphanage.

The golden frames with photographs of times long past captured her attention. Wedding photos, christenings, birthday parties. The daughter looked like her father while the son carried his mother's eyes and smile. No sign of a third child. Then, she remembered a lone photograph she caught a glimpse of in the small room that Mirela used to have as a dressing room. She was instructed by the daughter to avoid that room.

'My mother is very protective of her possessions. Better steer clear of it. No reason to enter that small grubby area. The cleaner came every Monday. My mother will want to sit by the door when she enters there to sweep and mop. She will probably ask you to follow the cleaner around and yes, she will mean it and wish for a full report,' the daughter had said over the phone.

But curiosity was always a weakness for Zoe. 'Your Achilles' Heel,' the head nun had once told her.

'My what?' seven-year-old Zoe had replied.

'Your Achilles' Heel. Your weak spot. You are too curious, child! And that sweet tooth of yours! Ts ts ts!' As the years went by, the nun had added, 'you are too gullible, child!' to the list.

Zoe was thinking of the warrior demigod Achilles and his vulnerable heel as she entered the *forbidden* room. The room's shutter on the lone window was permanently down preventing any sunrays entering. Zoe switched on the light and walked towards the dressing table with the large mirror above it. She picked up the oval silver frame and gazed at the small child in the photo. A happy smiling boy with dimples not older than two. 'May the Holy Mary bless your little heart up there, my angel.' Zoe crossed herself. 'What a shame. To die so young,' she whispered. She then knelt and bowed her head to pray. She wished to avoid questioning the Lord about His choices. The death of a child was something Zoe could not understand and how it fit in the grander scheme of things. 'Yes, yes, the Lord works in mysterious ways, but it would be nice to have some understanding at times like these,' she had once complained to a nun after a friend of hers in the orphanage passed away from an aggressive tumour at the age of nine. 'We are mere humans, Zoe. You think a God owes you an explanation? Do you explain everything you do to your cat? To the ants crawling by your window?' The nun's answer just confused her young mind more.

'Amen,' she said and stood up, placing the frame of Michael's photograph exactly back in place. The faint patch in the dust helped in her mission. Her fingers played around on the top drawer's handle. She opened it slightly, with care, without a sound. A large jewellery box with a red velvet lid stood out among brushes and brooches. Zoe looked behind her out of instinct. The booming TV informed her that there was not way Mirela could hear her. Zoe sat down on the floor and placed the heavy box on her lap. She gasped in excitement at the precious stones sparkling under the strong light. Zoe had only seen riches like these in store windows. She surely had never touched such pearls and diamonds before. The only thing that graced her body was a thin cheap chain around her neck that carried the little cross that the nuns gave as a gift to all the orphan girls. She picked up a gold ring with three red gems in a row nested upon it. It fitted her well. Zoe raised her hand to eye level and waved her fingers around. A twisted silver bracelet, representing an olive's branch, landed on her wrist, while Mirela's pearls fell upon her old necklace. The earrings took her longer to choose. She stood up and tried different ones as she smiled at herself in the mirror. 'Lady Zoe,' she joked and giggled. She stroked the pearly stones one by one.

The doorbell rang and made her jump. She realized that silence had returned to the house. The TV could no longer be heard. Panicked breathing kicked in as she frantically tidied up the valuables. With everything back in place - or so she thought, she rushed to the door. She was panting and sweating as she crossed the living room, hoping that no one would be at the door just like the times before.

The thinnest man Zoe had ever laid eyes upon stood in his post-office uniform, holding a square brown package in his arm. 'Good morning, little lady. I was told there was someone to open the door.' The dark figure came forward. The sun was behind him preventing Zoe to see the man clearly. His voice gave away his age before he took four steps forward. A white goatee and thinned-out grey hairs came into view as they both exchanged genuine Greek smiles. 'Do I have to sign somewhere?' Zoe asked taking the box from the man's stretched out arms. His uniform was worn-in and a round button hung on for dear life from a single thread. 'No need, Miss. I tend to deliver packages to the door as, believe or not, our area has seen many... robberies, let's say for lack of a better word. Things tend to go missing around these parts of the village.'

The package was lighter than its size would fool you into believing. Zoe placed it on the wooden cabinet to her side.

'Teenagers! They are the ones stealing, most likely. I think they come up here and ring the doorbell, too. Quite often, I may add!'

The man tilted his head and his pupils snuck into their corners. 'No teens around these parts, Miss. Maybe when visiting their grandma for some home baked moussaka on a Sunday. No, no. Things disappear around here. Poof.' He moved his hands around theatrically like a magician.

'What is this by the way?'

'Oh, Mrs. Mirela enjoys ordering from those annoying shopping channels. It could be literally anything. Glasses with a compass built in them or shoes that turn into drink shakers. And of course, all this weird crap on offer only for the next ten minutes!'

Zoe could not control her laughter. The man saluted her with his blue cap and whistling down the path, he returned to his minivan. Zoe closed the door, picked up the delivered box and examined it for a label. Nothing to reveal its contents. Shaking it did not help either. No rattling noise: it was packed well. *'Oh, well. Maybe she will open it in front of me.'*

Mirela sat up straight in bed, flicking through a weekly TV magazine. 'Good movie on today, child. Remind me to open this mind-numbing box at nine.'

'Yes, Mrs.' Zoe raised her hands. 'This came for you just now…'

'Yes, yes. I heard you flirting with Thomas. That old fart still thinks he is a catch. Ever since his wife died, he is more cheery with the opposite sex.'

'Cheerier,' Zoe corrected her in her mind. She left the box by Mirela's side. 'I'm sure he is just lonely and wishes to have someone to talk to.'

Mirela sniggered. 'Gullible, foolish child. Men's Achilles' heel is between your innocent legs, dear.'

Zoe's neck muscles tensed up and vibrated. Again, she felt uncomfortable around Mirela. Her words were like a vacuum of joy, sucking happy feelings down to an abyss to be lost forever and spreading darkness all around. But Zoe stood there, her curiosity getting the best of her. 'So, what's in the box, Mrs?' Suddenly, Mirela reached out and grabbed her hand. She squeezed it with strength and pulled it close.

'You're hurting me.'

'That's my ring! You dirty little thief. Come in here with a pair of knickers to your name and take my ring!'

Zoe looked down at the bright red stones shining on her finger. The postman had made her forget to take it off. 'It... it was my grandma's,' Zoe lied. 'So, you have a similar one, Mrs? Do you want me to fetch it for you?'

'It's mine!' Mirela was screaming. 'Bring me a knife and I will take it back, finger and all.'

Zoe struggled to pull free. Mirela was stronger than what appearances would lead you to believe. 'Let go of me, Mrs.' Mirela grunted like a wild animal, opening her mouth, and coming closer. 'I will bite it off! It's mine!' Zoe panicked at the thought. She used her free hand to push the woman back and leaned back to fall on the floor. On the ground she quickly took off the ring. 'Here, look. It's going back to its place. I am no thief, ma'am. I was cleaning and I apologise, I was tempted to try it on, and the doorbell rang...'

'Just fuck off and put it back, sneaky rat!'

Zoe ran out the door as tears snaked down her flushed cheeks. She could not stop shaking her head. She had blown her chance of having a home. A job. Purpose. 'Then again, who wants to work for that rude, cursing witch!' She took off the ring and just before placing it back in place, she read

the inscription on the inside. 'For Katerina, my love! 1991.'
She left the ring exactly where she had found it. But she
could not resist the impulse. She began turning bracelets
upside down and looking inside the other rings. Not all had
a message. Yet, on the inside of a platinum bracelet she
read, 'Helen, you are my rock. Always have been and
always will be.'

Zoe tidied up and went back to her room. She needed
her pillow. She needed a proper cry. She needed Leo. After
wiping away gathered tears, she picked up her phone. 'A
message from Leo!' She sat up and smiled, her mouth
welcoming salty rivulets. 'Hey sweet cake, how is Corfu?
Settled in? I miss you terribly! I have tomorrow night off.
Shall I drive to the port and head over?'

'Night off!' Zoe rolled her eyes and her fingers joined to
form fists. She started typing, mumbling the words as she
went along with her rant. 'Night off? You're still with her?
Your wife still controlling your life? This is why I left.
Because you didn't have the balls to leave. To leave her and
be with me...' She stopped and gasped for air. She stared at
the message and remembered all his sweet talk. What was
the point? She was only setting herself up to receive a ton
of his usual excuses. She deleted the message and sat on the
edge of the bed. She held her head and continued with her
cleansing cry. She never knew that he was married. Not in
the beginning. He was a kind professor at her university and
Zoe was not use to male attention. He became her first and
then the truth was revealed. He swore he was getting a
divorce and that for the last year, he was basically separated
from his wife. Cliché or not, Zoe needed him. Stability, love,
compassion, attention, money. He meant more to her that
he could ever had imagined. She fell for his lie. She waited.
She waited until she could not bear to wait anymore. The

job came as a release from his hold. But now, as she sat sobbing and panting, she wanted him near, to get lost in his embrace. 'If Mirela fires me, I will need him more than ever.'

Zoe stood up and decided to face the music. Metaphorically and literally. Greek island music exited Mirela's room and travelled down the hallway. As Zoe got closer, she could hear Mirela trying to snap her fingers along with the beat, singing breathlessly with her croaky voice. She stood by the door, waiting for her patient to notice her. Mirela turned toward her and smiled. 'I love this music. They don't make them like they used.'

'No, they do not.'

'Lunch time already, Alice? What have you prepared for me today?'

Zoe walked into the room and approached the bed. 'I'm not your daughter, Mrs. It's me. Zoe. Your nurse.'

Mirela's face darkened and her fingers crawled along the sheets to find the remote. She switched off the music and said, 'Yes, yes. Of course. Alice never visits anymore. She has her own life. I am imprisoned here. Unable to move, to live.'

'It is early for lunch. I haven't started yet. Would you prefer a snack? Cut up some nice summer fruit?'

Mirela nodded. 'You're my cook?'

'And nurse. I will be taking good care of you.'

'You live here?'

'Since yesterday, Mrs. I'm Zoe.'

Mirela looked around the room. 'Yes, yes. You are. Go for the fruit now, girl.'

Zoe rushed out of the room and once in the corridor, danced. 'She forgot about the ring!' She picked up her phone and began to type. 'Hi, Leo. Looking forward to seeing you tomorrow night. Come late after my lady is asleep. I'm sending you the pinpoint on google maps. Wait outside until I say so.' She reread the message. 'Good! No sweet talk. If he hasn't moved out, I'll break it off.' She exhaled heavily, crossed herself and went into the kitchen to cut strawberries, watermelon, and peaches into small enough pieces for Mirela to chew.

After lunch that day, Mirela took her pills and had a bad case of nausea. Zoe gave her a pain killer and broke half a sedative in her patient's water and watched her drift away to dream land.

Zoe found herself with time. She decided to keep herself -and her curiosity- busy by staying out of the house. She wore an old pair of tracksuit bottoms and a black tank top that was ripped on the bottom and had a tiny hole that Zoe found cute near her breasts. She walked over to the stone shed and was glad to find the green wooden door unlocked. A small spade, a garden fork, a hoe with a dark-wood handle, a trowel and a rake all sat in the corner neglected. Spider webs filled up the space between them. Zoe wore the pair of kitchen gloves, thinking of her nails and Leo's visit the following day. Zoe exited the shed, various tools in hand, and turned around to catch a glimpse of herself in the dusty shed windows. 'Well, well, well. Come on, Gertrude Jekyll, let's get to work!'

She whistled a pop song (out of tune as always) as she went along the pathway, pulling out stubborn summer weeds. 'If only you produced a beautiful flower or nut or fruit,' she said and then stopped. 'How selfish of us humans. No need for something, so kill it. It's in our way of what we consider beauty. They are out of order. In the wrong place,' she mumbled. She let out a quiet laugh. 'Zoe the philosopher, all right. Rationally reasoning the existence of weeds! Analysing the selfishness in humans!' She continued her weed massacre all the way down to the main gate. As she turned her back to the metallic entrance to look back at her hard work accomplishment, she noticed a shadow growing beneath her feet. A figure of a person. The hairs on the back of her neck shot up and she let out a small gasp as swung around to see a tall woman starting right behind her.

'Oh, child, no need to worry. This isn't the big city. All friendly folk outside of these gates,' the woman in the flowery blue dress said with a happy rhythm to her soothing voice. 'I live just there,' she said, pointing to a renovated two-storey house with a wooden balcony and a stone wall running around the property. A row of lemon trees in the back provided shade to the well-maintained grass. 'Your nearest neighbor.'

'I'm Zoe. I am here to work as a nurse for Mrs. Mirela.'

The woman raised her eyebrows. 'Yes, of course. We can't have the killer suffering now, can we?'

Zoe dusted off her dirty hands on her clothes. '*Did I hear correctly?*' Zoe remained lost for words as the chatty woman continued talking about the weather, applauding her garden work and the village in general. The woman kept on staring at Zoe's gloves. 'Take them off, dear. Not good for the hands. Our skin needs to breath. Take it from me. I am sixty-two next month. You wouldn't tell, would you?'

'No, no,' Zoe quickly agreed, taking off her gloves. The woman's stare never left Zoe's hands. She seemed disappointed. She frowned and stopped talking. She looked around her and took a step closer to Zoe.

'The postman said you were wearing a ring today. A

golden one with three red gems on it,' she whispered into Zoe's ear.

Zoe took a step back. 'Err… yeah… err… it was not mine. I should not have been wearing it.'

'I know well that it is not yours. Did you find it in Mirela's things?'

Zoe looked back at the house. 'I should be getting back. My patient might need be. I'm too far away as to hear her.'

The woman with the dyed blonde hair crossed her arms. 'You need to tell me the truth, girl. That old witch has been stealing our stuff for years. We need proof. She can't get away with every crime.'

Zoe shook her head. 'Mrs. Mirela is a wealthy woman. She has no need to steal.'

'Kleptomaniacs with a weakness for fine jewelry are usually rich, believe it or not.'

Zoe continued shaking her head in disbelief. 'She is bed ridden. She can't even walk!'

'She walked just fine up until a couple of years ago. I never believed it. She just wanted to keep her poor son close. That's my ring by the way.'

Just then, the doorbell rang. Zoe turned toward the house. The bell rang again, yet no one stood at the door.

'I should be getting back,' Zoe said and dashed away along the path, wiping her sweaty forehead and panting. *What the heck?*

'The name's Katerina, by the way. Nice to meet you, nurse!'

Zoe stepped into the house and closed the door behind her. Breathless, she slid down the wall and sat down on the floor. She placed her hand upon her heart. 'Killer? She said killer, right? Kleptomaniac? Oh, Zoe, what have you gone and gotten yourself into this time?'

Zoe performed a trick taught to her by the head nun from her youth. 'Freeze your mind. Pray, ask for strength, then stop thinking about everything and get on with your chores. No point in overthinking things. You will get nothing done!' the petite nun with the wrinkly face and the sharp emerald eyes had advised her. Zoe went about with her new routine. Hours later as she turned off Mirela's chandelier and placed her night light on the floor behind the bedside table, she exhaled in relief. She had managed to keep her thoughts at bay. 'But tomorrow, I think I need to go for a walk through the village and really find out who my patient truly is.'

After her shower, she laid upon her bed and picked up her phone. Just a single text from Leo about how excited he was about the following night. Nothing from Mirela's daughter. Nothing from her son. 'No wonder she is so bitter. But as soon as she dies, I bet they will be first at the attorney's office to get the will opened!'

An hour later, her eyes were tearing up from staring at the bright cell screen for so long. She could not read anymore lifestyle articles and switched to videos with humorous cats and dogs. Her eyelids retaliated and ventured down. Just as Zoe found that perfect spot on her pillow, she heard the light switch in the corridor. '*Not again!*' Zoe sat up and turned on her nightstand lamp. 'No such things as ghosts. No one in the house!' She spoke to give herself confidence. 'It must be some sort of electrical damage or malfunction. Bells and lights and crap.' She got up, locked her door, and returned to bed. 'Freeze your mind! Good night!'

Chapter Six

'So, we are finally getting to the final day?'

Damien scratched his short nails into the wood of the chair in which he sat uncomfortably as he tried -and failed- to find a spot more congenial for his behind.

'In a rush, Lieutenant?'

Damien took in her smile. There was something about the woman before him when she smiled. It lit up her face. Gave it a certain glow. Especially when her eyes were focused on him. His nails dug deeper. He had not been looked at that way since her. *Her*. He dared not say her name. His soul could not bear to hear it even in his mind. His heart had shrivelled up and broke long ago, and yet it managed an extra beat with Zoe's smile.

'Well, all I have are names of dead bodies which you gave us on your way here. I know who the deceased are, I have a forensics team at the house collecting evidence, two coroners performing autopsies...'

'And you are here.'

'Exactly. I have an eyewitness. You have all I need.'

'Do I now?' Another smile. Another extra beat. Another rant inside his head to focus; to control his frailty for a pretty woman. A siren roared to life outside as an ambulance took off on its way to save an obese middle-aged Greek male that ate and drank too much the night before. His heart had awoken him in the worse possible way. The blaring noise interrupted Damien's inner rant and returned his attention to the hospital room and the nurse lying in bed. 'So, final day.'

'I woke up and took a look outside my window. The sun was generous to the village and its surrounding meadows. I felt happy inside. Warm. I would not have ever guessed of the events that were to follow.'

Damien placed his hand upon hers. Intention, instinct, professional courtesy, witness psychology. He was not sure what urged the spontaneous move.

Suddenly, Zoe's pupils rose and only white now occupied her eye sockets. A twitch took over her neck veins and her head began to vibrate. In a matter of two seconds, her entire body was shaking violently upon the bed. Machinery around her started to beep. Damien rushed to the door, pushing it open. 'Help! We need some help in here! Now!'

Two nurses, followed by a doctor, sprinted by him. 'Stay here,' the bald doctor ordered without turning to face him. Damien walked up to the swinging door and held it still. He pressed his nose upon the small square window and attempted to see through the glass blocks. He bit his lower lip and cursed, not sure if the vulgar words came from his anger of not getting the full story or from the fact that he found himself caring about the young woman's well-being.He caught mingled words from the sizeable gap between the two thick doors. '*A seizure? Come on, Zoe!*' Damien held back his fists. The wall was not his enemy, even if his knuckles were used to being bloody and sore. He walked off his nerves in anticipation of the doctor's exit from the room.

'Is she okay? What is wrong with her?'

'It's a seizure, officer,' the doctor replied much calmly than him.

'What caused it? Is this all too much for her?'

'We haven't got her full history. The nuns emailed us an incomplete medical file from the doctor that oversaw the orphanage. Not very thorough with the orphans it seems. She could be epileptic. Or yes, it could have been from the stress of the awful... events and the interrogation. She has no fever, so I have ordered a toxicology report.'

'Drugs?'

'Maybe. Could just be a blood sugar count matter. For the time being, let her rest.'

Damien exited the hospital defeated and disappointed in himself.

Chapter Seven

Damien slammed down on the brakes hard. His tires produced an ear-piercing screeching sound that gathered many stares at the intersection. The rangy woman with the long curly ginger hair stood inches away from his car with eyes wide open. Her hands held on tightly to her baby's blue stroller. Her older son hid behind her, showing the lieutenant his middle finger. Damien considered himself a dexterous driver. Even when drunk. Now, sober, he blamed his anger. That and the fact that his right hand was looking for the whisky bottle below his seat while his left hand multitasked by holding both his phone and the steering wheel. He was texting the coroner that he was on his way. If his eyewitness needed rest, he did not. He could not swallow the fact that it had been hours since the crime and he still did not have the full story. 'You fucking idiot. You saw a pretty damsel in distress and sat by her side like a worried lover and forgot to do your duty! Twat!'

He was not the only one cursing him.

The woman pulled herself out of the shock and began shouting at him.

'It's a crossing, you lunatic! You could have killed us, you freaking maniac!'

Damien mouthed 'I'm sorry' many times with his hand upon his chest and watched as the family of three walked over to the safety of the sidewalk. At a much lower speed, he continued his short journey to the police morgue. He drove down the busy street at the only pace Corfu did. Slow. He was glad for the newly built underground parking of the large government building block that housed an array of services ranging from a court to a police department to a property and vehicle cadaster. The police morgue was last on the entry sign.

The morgue was also underground. Just above the parking. Hidden below the police department's forensics lab. Damien took the stairs. He hated elevators. Despised their confined space and stale air. Born and raised on the island, he did not have the need to use them often. Few buildings in Corfu had more then four floors. You could count them on your two hands.

Damien stood in front of the mirror in the hallway and patted down his clothes. He fixed his belt, bringing the silver buckle to the center. He ran his fingers through his hair and along his neat eyebrows. The main medical examiner was an elderly man just a step away from retirement, but his trainee and assistant were not. Both were young and both were women. Damien walked in with his back straight and with a bright smile upon his face. 'Good day to you all.'

Neither returned his smile and only the medical examiner replied to his greeting. 'What's good about it?' he grunted and pointed to the row of dead bodies lying on metallic tables. 'I've been working my wrinkly ass off since yesterday!'

'Now that's painted a pretty picture in my mind.'

'Want to see more pretty images, Lieutenant?' the man said and pulled back the sheet on the second body. It was the body found down in the mansion's empty cellar. The only one that was not fresh. The victim that outdated the rest.

'So, doc? What you got for me?' Damien asked taking a step closer, playing it cool. He could see the Y-section on the body. The recent red marks upon the pale dead skin.

'Well, you were nearly right about the time of death. It is over a month old.' The doctor raised the dead male's top lip and then pointed to his hand. 'Nails have fallen out but not all. The body has begun to liquify, but is still in early stages. Five or six weeks.'

'Cause of death?'

The doctor had his mouth buried deep in behind his elbow and was coughing rhythmically trying to clear his throat. A heavy smoker with a passion for not quitting, you could hear the air struggling to rise and exit his thin lips.

'Damien, a hand please.' The doctor placed both his hands on the body's shoulder and lifted him up slowly while Damien quickly pulled on two rubber gloves and helped the examiner turn the male victim onto his side. 'Two stab wounds to the back. Here and here.' The blood lines had faded in color and looked so innocent on the young man's pale back. Small. Just a few inches wide. As if incapable of bringing on death. 'Kitchen knife is my educated guess. Sharp and slim. No teeth.' The doctor let go of the body and Damien gently rested him back in position. 'The beheading happened post-mortem. From the marks, I'll take an educated guess and say by a saw. Did you find the head?'

Damien shook his head. 'The forensic team swept the entire property well. Nothing.' Damien formed a fist and covered his mouth as he coughed. 'Anything note-worthy about the rest?'

'All murdered around the same hour.'

Damien nodded. 'Yes, the survivor said much. They all killed each other, she said.'

'Now that's a story…'

'Yeah. Still waiting for the full picture. Girl is traumatized…'

'Aren't we all? Well, I don't know what your living one is telling you, but I can fill you in on what my dead ones are telling me. The man lost his hand while alive. A butcher's cleaver. Cut straight off. The daughter's hair was covered in the man's blood. I'm guessing he ran towards her when he lost it. Maybe she was his attacker?'

'He was the nurse's lover. From the forensic photos and the blood spatter on the bedroom walls, I would say that they were most likely on the bed when he was attacked.'

'What a way to go. He then received the fatal blow in the stomach. Same weapon. The daughter died from a deep stab wound to the chest, most likely from the house's kitchen knife. Similar wound to the one-month-old body of the basement.'

'What about the lady of the house?'

'What a diseased-riddled body that was. That one was a fighter; I can tell you that much.' The doctor walked over to the first body in line, pulled back the white sheet down to the chest and turned Mirela's head to the side. 'Heavy blow to the back. She fell back on something hard. Wooden furniture?'

Damien nodded. 'Yep. Big blood spot on the corner of a

large antique sideboard in the hallway. Right next to her body.'

'What a night,' the medical examiner said, laying back the sheet, trudging over to his seat and falling back into it. He scratched the back of his head and stared at the lieutenant. 'So?'

'So?'

'What's the story here? The line of death? Come on. Share. I know that overanalytical mind of yours has played the scene over a hundred times in your mind.'

Damien scratched his short beard and walked over to the coroner. He looked to his side to see what his two assistants were up to. One sat in front of her computer screen and was processing data, while the other, the one with the kind honey eyes, stood by some weird looking equipment in the corner and was weighing stuff Damien would rather not know what it was. He raised his voice. He loved an audience. Especially a female one.

'Well, based on the evidence, I could see how it played out. Having a survivor and knowing there was no attacker helps. It all happened between the group. The only thing I am not sure about is how the body in the basement fits in. Did someone discover him and that set in motion the tragic events of the night? Is his death unrelated to the massacre?' Damien asked and shrugged his broad shoulders. 'If you want a good tale to rest your mind until the full story, then I would say that the daughter, for whatever reason, attacked the nurse's lover. Maybe she thought he was an intruder? A naked stranger in her mother's mansion? That is why she was carrying the knife and cleaver. The nurse sees the attack and jumps to his defense. The mother intervenes somehow.'

'Somehow?'

'She is bed-ridden. Hasn't walked in ages. It must have

taken terrible strength to have taken those few steps from her room to the hallway. The two women are fighting above the dying man that crawled back to the room, leaving his hand behind. He was probably going for the phone but bled out before calling the police. The mother gets pushed out the way and bangs her head. The daughter tried to stab the nurse but the nurse, after being stabbed in the leg, fights back and stabs the daughter in the chest. The police arrive and she runs out to safety.'

The doctor whistled and scratched his face. Both women were looking over. 'What a story,' one mumbled to the other.

'One that I need to confirm!'

After the morgue, Damien drove back home with Jolie on his mind. The canine came running and hopped around him as he entered his apartment. She recognized the specific rattling of his keys and awoke in a split second. 'Ready for a walk? Huh? Wanna go for a walk, baby?' Just the mention of the word had her barking happily. Her nails scratched the tiles as she danced at the sight of her green lead.

The air was stale compared to the fresh air outside and carried smells of alcohol, crisps, leftover pizza and dog piss. 'One minute, girl.' Damien dashed down the hallway and opened the kitchen window by a few inches. He did the same with his bedroom window that had a view of the park opposite. It was a school day, and the place of greenery was quiet much to Damien's delight. He could let Jolie have a nice run around.

Jolie would never go far from him. He was her constant. Her stable. She would sniff along the dirt path but always looked behind her to check that he was still there, sitting on the bench on the shade. She found a piece of wood and picked it up. She brought it back to him. 'Wanna play, huh? Bad daddy, didn't buy you a ball?' He stroked her head. After a few throws, she placed her head on his knee. Her tongue hung out and she breathed rapidly. The game was over. He scratched her ear and kissed her on her head. He gazed at the endless flow of cars and people in the streets surrounding the park. 'There really is no point in life, my dear. Zero. Nothing at all. I'm tired. Fed up. If nothing changes, when you die, I'll follow you.'

Chapter Eight

The small brown mouse was alone for the first time in its short life. Its whiskers shook in the air as it spread them apart. He was hungry. Leaving the family nest is a hard test for all species. Especially when forced to do so due to the poison laid out by the old man that lived next door to the police station in Corfu. A common house mouse, he was used to being a part of a group. He journeyed through the old walls with his huge black eyes wide open, carefully planning each next step. He nibbled on a piece of torn fabric before turning his attention to the delicious mixture of aromas floating through the stale air enclosed inside the concrete beams. It originated from a tiny hole just meters away from him. He ran to the light. Loud noises and movements prevented him from dashing out into the open. But the voices calmed down as Anneta sat back into her red office chair and took a big bite out of her donut. Cliché for a cop but she did not mind. She lived to serve her sweet tooth. Merenda chocolate, crepes and donuts satisfied her stomach, even though she hated how they sat on her bum and lingered around her waist. '*Oh well, we cannot have it all,*' she thought and took another bite.

Drops of frosting fell to the floor. She looked down on all the paperwork that had ganged up on her desk. Witness statements from the senior residents of the street leading up to Mirela's mansion. She began to gather them as to read them again and sort them for filing when she noticed movement by her right foot. Hungry for food and starving for adventure, the little rotten beast and his little beating heart, took the plunge. He ran out and picked up the sugary treat.

Anneta hated the expression 'screamed at the top of her lungs', but that is how she described to her mother later that day the cry that came out of her mouth when she witnessed the furry beast nibbling by her feet.

Anneta leapt onto her chair while throwing all the statements up into the air. Everything around her had turned into white noise. She could not hear her colleagues asking what was going on. Colors faded around her as all she could see was the brown mouse fleeing towards the hole in the wall.

'Mouse,' she finally managed to say. 'A fucking huge mouse!'

The station's Captain was notorious about his laziness. He was a good officer in his youth and was a skillful leader in handing out assignments and positions to the correct people, but he did love his office chair way too much. Everyone knew that if you needed him, you went to him. It was law that you only 'annoyed' him, if needed. Most only saw him as he came in late in the morning and left early in the evening. His armchair at home was more comfortable than his office chair and Netflix on his plasma TV surely tramped YouTube on his smart phone. No one judged him for this. He was nine months away from retirement. He had done enough. It was shameful how the austerity measures pushed retirement ages upwards. The general consensus was that he should be at home relaxing, enjoying his garden, his grandkids and taking cruises with his wife.

Captain Demetriou dropped his phone as the screaming startled him. His heavy body rocked in his frail chair, and he jumped forward. He rushed outside and pushed open his glass door. 'What the...?'

Anneta felt like a fool even though she argued with her inner voice that it was a mouse. 'A freaking mouse! By my foot!'

'Okay, dear. Calm down,' the captain said. He raised his hand. 'Phillip,' he called over a young cadet. 'Get Helen to call maintenance and get that hole closed. Then book an exterminator for the walls. Book them for Sunday when most of us are off.'

'Aye, Captain,' the man with the baby face replied and rushed over to Helen, the police station's receptionist.

'So, what's all this?' he inquired as he towered Anneta who had dropped to all fours and was gathering the scattered pieces of paper.

'All out of order!' She felt like screaming again. 'Witness statements, Chief. The whole street had nothing and something to say. All just wanted to tell us that they heard screams and that they disliked the mansion's owner with a passion. They all wanted confirmation that she had indeed died.'

The captain scratched his thick black moustache. His hair might have thinned and whitened but the hairs above his thick lip, still made him proud. Made him feel young and manly. 'I see.'

He took a step closer to her as she stood up.

'And how's Damien?'

Anneta tightened her grip on the renegade papers and gave the same awkward smile that she gave her father when she was caught smelling of cigarettes as a teen. 'He's doing good. Working the case. He is handling the survivor and today he visited the coroner. Busy, busy, busy.' The entire sentence came out in one breath.

'Hmm. I see.'

Anneta sat back down and lowered her head in the papers. She wasn't reading, just waiting for the captain to return to his cave. He did not. She could feel him towering over her; his shadow grew upon the papers as he came closer and blocked the ceiling light. 'I admire you for not bad-mouthing him.' The captain spoke quieter than usual. 'I know it is hard being his partner, especially being a woman and all. I imagine you do not think highly of him.'

'Not one to judge, Chief.'

'I know him well. You need not explain anything to me or see it as ratting on him to the boss. All am asking is if he is controlling the alcohol. The debts and the women and the partying are his problem. But a drunk officer not able to give his one-hundred percent is my issue.'

Anneta swung her chair around. 'He may drink like a motherfucker without a care in the world, but he has never ever shown up drunk at a case. Hungover? Of course. That's his norm. But he always makes sense, and can I be frank, sir?' She waited for her captain to nod. 'He is a remarkable detective. I truly do not understand why he lives this way. He could have been one of the greats. And not only at work. A family man...'

The captain raised his palm and exhaled. 'I know this all too well, child. He has too much grief in him that one. He drinks to keep her out of his head.'

'Who?'

'Continue the good work, Sergeant. And do not hesitate to knock on my door if you feel like your partner is spiraling out of control. I am here to help. Not punish.'

And with that, he trudged back to his lair.

'*Her?*'

Chapter Nine

I hope you never have to phone a public service number in Greece. The odds on receiving a reply are thin, thinner than a new-born moon. The chances of getting served and helped by the first person whose voice you heard are on par with winning the National Lottery. Hospitals gave you the best chances in the public sector. That did not prevent Damien from wasting half an hour of his life trying to locate a doctor that could give him an update on Zoe's condition. A head nurse though, came to his rescue. She had overheard the young nurse trying to locate the on-call doctor on the floor.

'Who is asking?'

The young nurse asked Damien to hold for a second and placed her right hand on the telephone. 'The Lieutenant in charge of the case, Mrs. Voula,' she whispered.

'Give him to me.' Voula spoke with the only way she knew. With authority and with her bosom and nose up high. 'Sir? Hello. This is the head nurse. Your victim? The young woman with the stab wound? Yes, she had another episode. She has been sedated to help her remain calm. Poor thing needs to rest. The doctor would know more but I can assure you all tests needed have been ordered and are underway. She will be fine, sir. She is in the best hands on the island. Maybe if it isn't that important, you could come by in the morning? Visiting hours begin at eight.'

Damien ground his teeth. The nurse reminded him of his late aunt Vaso. She spoke a hundred words per minute in the same rhythm. A rhythm you knew was unacceptable to interrupt. He listened while shaking his head.

He only managed one word. 'Fine.' And the call ended. He missed telephones from his childhood. He missed the pleasure of slamming down the receiver. No such rapture from chucking your mobile into the passenger seat.

'Back to the station it is.'

He parked in his allocated spot by the old stone wall, switched off the vehicle's engine and sat there staring at the wall. The station was a cage for him. The uniform suffocated him. He felt like a wild animal, trapped, and forced to perform circus tricks. He regretted his career choice within the first two years. A young man with his urges, forced to wake up before the sun and help out with traffic at the town's main roundabout. Then, the long walks placing parking tickets and arguing with angry locals. Inside the station, boredom attacked. The same mindless, pointless conversations about football and politics. Greek males' hot topics for the last one-hundred and fifty years. He wanted out. He signed up to study criminology and law at Corfu's open university. He worked the lessons around his schedule. He knew he wanted to be working homicide. To be like the detectives on his favorite British and American TV shows.

To throw the uncomfortable and plain ugly uniform off his body. To be out in the field investigating rather than cooped up inside the miserable walls that enclosed his pathetic co-workers.

For years he praised his choices to better himself with a finer education.

Now, he was not so sure.

University brought her into his life. Meeting her brought the pain. The pain brought the alcohol. Maybe he should have stayed an ignorant yet blissful traffic warden. Maybe.

He finally opened his car door. He lit a cigarette and smoked it while leaning on his vehicle. 'You're stalling, mate. Get your ass to work. Go fill in the paperwork. Oh, pure joy, oh the ecstasy...' His bud was exterminated below his shoe as he took the first step to go inside. He looked back and chuckled at the patch his body had cleaned on his dusty car. He fixed his messy hair and walked straight in. A bee line to Anneta's desk. 'Hey partner, anything interesting with the witnesses' statements?'

Anneta looked up at him. She wasn't expecting to see him. She sat up straight and repeated what she had said to the captain not long ago. 'The whole street had nothing and something to say. All just wanted to tell us that they heard screams and that they disliked the mansion's owner with a passion. They all wanted confirmation that she had died.' She held back a smile. She impressed herself with her memory. The exact words were repeated.

'No details that could help? Even the slightest thread to pull on? Nothing interesting at all?' Damien sat down upon her desk.

She shook her head. 'All were sleeping. All of them. Old folks and all. They woke up by the woman's screams at exactly the same time. Some called the police. None exited their houses and said they did not see anything from the windows.'

Damien was scratching his jaw when she asked him about the autopsies.

'In line with the theories we discussed on the night. I will have the full story though as soon as the nurse is feeling better and up to further interrogation.' More face scratching followed. 'Why did they hate her so much? And if the neighbors loathed her, what about her kids? The nurse? Could her backstory have any significance?'

'Could explain the viciousness behind certain blows but the nurse claims self-defense on her part...'

'Damn seizures...'

'Excuse me?'

He waved his hand. 'Nothing. I hate waiting.' He was scratching his hands, intertwining his fingers.

'Fancy a cigarette break round the back?' Anneta built up the courage to ask. She never thought that she would wish to hang around with her partner, but her curiosity -as always- got the best of her.

Damien looked puzzled. Anneta enjoyed the occasional smoke when others headed outside but she was what most would call a social smoker than a dedicated hard chain smoker like he was. And a cigarette was not what he was craving at the moment. Her next words filled in the awkward silence and shocked him as it was as if she was reading his mind. Could his partner have figured him out better than what he thought?

'There's a small bottle of Ouzo hidden in the freezer if you like a shot or two?'

The dark alley behind the station was a secret heaven for the officers on duty. Closed off from their parking lot, it welcomed no vehicles or passers by. It led to a dead end; the back brick wall of the high street's new bakery. Away from nosy eyes, the officers could enjoy some fresh air on their break. Fresh air. Their code for smoking. None bothered to beautify the area and maybe that was a part of its charm. No forced pots and plants and flowers and shrubs. Just some old wooden chairs upon cement surrounded by bricks housing mold.

The shot went down nicely, icing his throat as it descended. The alcohol kick brought a faint smile upon his face. He lit his and her cigarettes. Anneta blew out a small cloud of smoke and went in for the kill.

'I've never been one to beat around the bush, so I am just going to throw some thoughts off my mind and take it the right way, okay?'

Damien chuckled. 'I'm not the type you approve off.'

'It's not that. Well, not exactly. I've only been here for a year. Homicides and investigations were my goal from day one at police academy. Being sent off to the furthest island from home and being paired up with you was not a part of the dream. Maybe I had idealized way too many cop pairings in all those TV shows but a partner that seems more interested in drinking himself senseless and banging cheap whores was definitely not what I was expecting.' She paused as if expecting him to interrupt her by now. 'However, even though I feel ignored in the process, I cannot say you are bad at what you do. You observe details that others miss, you give your all until you get to the bottom of things and for some bizarre reason, all other police officers, the captain included, love you, respect you and I can see the sorrow in their eyes when they see what you have become. So that has led me to the conclusion that you weren't always like this. You were that type of partner I longed for. And I know a woman is to be blamed. And it is none of my fucking business, but what happened, dude? What screwed you up so much? Maybe if I knew then I could accept you and maybe you could finally see me and throw me a bone every now and then. Work with me...'

Out of breath, she paused.

'You make it sound like there is some sort of great mystery. Never crossed your mind that maybe I just grew up into an asshole? A miserable cunt that has zero joy in life except this?'

'Not by yourself.'

Damien threw his cigarette to the ground and poured himself another shot of Ouzo. It vanished in a second. 'What is it you want, Anneta? My sad backstory? For what? To help you feel pity for me as to fit the mold of the broken hero?'

'Help me understand you.'

Damien shook his head. 'It makes me sound weak. Boohoo. He had a crap life, so he drinks. Many have been through worse.'

'We all deal with shit in different ways' She looked down at her feet. A few leaves blew by her black shoes. 'I was raped in high school.' The words that came out so easily shocked her. She had never uttered those words before, to anyone.

Damien's stern expression softened. 'What?' He took a step forward and placed his hand on her shoulder. She shook it straight off. 'Hey! No sympathy, right? No feeling pity, right? Our backstory is no excuse. It's a part of who we are. You wonder why I look at you disapprovingly. I hate drinking. I hate alcohol. I got drunk once in my life, once, and I was raped by a classmate of mine who thought I was as easy as the neighborhood prostitute that all the seniors visited back then. See? It doesn't make me a broken hero, but it helps you understand where I am coming from. Help me understand you.'

Damien exhaled and wandered up to the brick wall. 'Nicely played, partner.' He ran his fingers through his hair and sat down upon a hard wooden chair with a chipped back. He lit another cigarette. 'I'm no storyteller so don't expect much.' He stalled his story by skillfully blowing out three smoke rings in a row. 'My biological father fucked off when I was three. He vanished as to avoid paying for shit. We never heard from him again. I looked him up after I became a cop. He died working as a fisherman on the island of Rhodes. Mum was a violent psychopath. She used to burn me with her cigarettes when I was naughty. As naughty as a four-year-old kid could be. She used to place me in the bathtub for hours when she brought a date over for dinner and sex. I had to be really quiet as she never told her long line of lovers that she had a kid. As I grew up, I just wandered the streets. As a teen I got up to everything normal parents wished their offspring would never do. Mine was delighted to have the house to herself. She died of a heroin overdose a week before I turned sixteen. That's when my grandma entered my life. She was a saint. She had no idea where her daughter had been since running away from home at eighteen. Social services showed up at her village one day and told her she had a grandkid in Corfu. She sold her remaining livestock and left the farm to come to me. Strong-willed old Greek grandmother, you can imagine. She had me on the right track in a matter of days. My grades went up, my bad habits went out. Best two years of my life up to then and a week before my graduation, she was murdered.'

'Murdered?'

Damien nodded and flicked his cigarette. Another one

landed immediately in its place. He stared into the lighter's flame for a couple of seconds before lighting it. 'Stabbed and left to die in an alley similar to this one behind the marketplace down by the bay. Police were clueless. I had just turned eighteen. I sold my grandma's farm and my mum's house and set off to Athens for Police Academy. Not knowing who killed her was eating me up inside. It made no sense. Police said it was most likely a mugging. Years later, looking through the case, I came across a testimonial given by an eyewitness. The man said he saw a dodgy foreigner lurking around the old market. An Albanian, he stated, looking at old ladies' purses. He gave a description and everything, and even said that he last saw the low-life -his words, not mine- being shooed away just as my grand-mother was leaving the place. I recognized the witness's name. A total scumbag. My mum's last boyfriend. One hell of a violent asshole. The one she used to shoot up with. His statement was full of holes, and he was the only one that saw this foreign guy lurking around? No way. Anyway, long story short and all, he was the one that stabbed my grand-mother. My mother had promised him our family home. She was going to sign over our house for him to keep providing her with drugs. He told my granny that he had her word and that the house was his. He wanted her and me out by the end of the week. My grandma laughed in his face. He got rough and as she pushed to get away, he stabbed her. He was not one to control his rage. That was it. Homicides had won me over.' Another bud fell to the ground. 'We should be getting back. I need to call the hospital for an update.'

'Wait. That's not the whole story.'

Damien frowned. 'Told you, I'm no storyteller.'

'Yeah, but you left out the most important part.'

'Which is?'

'The woman that drove you to late nights, booze and paid sex.'

'Life drove me to late nights, booze and sex. Besides, I hardly ever pay.' They shared a laugh.

Anneta leaned back on the brick wall. 'Life's a bitch? That's it?'

'The universe well seems to hate me. Took my father, then my mother, then my grandmother. All seemed pretty pointless to me but hey, I was breathing and focused on solving cases. Thought to give peace of mind to victims' relatives as the resolution of my grandmother's death satisfied me. But then the universe took my only love away from me. And then I just didn't care anymore. I'm just killing time until the cosmos decides to kill me as well.'

'Where did you meet her?'

Damien smiled. It was a rare genuine smile. Anneta could feel the warmth it emitted. 'On a case. She worked on the same floor as a victim at an insurance company. She did the logistics. Smart girl. Pretty eyes. She floated magically into the room. I always had a weakness for girls with sexy cat-like eyes since high school. I could not take my eyes off her. I am not ashamed to say, I stalked her.' Damien chuckled. 'Not in that creepy sense. I just wandered outside her office building around closing hour hoping to bump into her. Coffee followed. Love came after. We moved in together. And the universe gave me another two great years before deciding again that that was enough. That was my limit it seemed. A few years of a father, a couple with a grandma and two with a lover. In September she found out she was pregnant, in October she found out she had pancreatic cancer. She had to get an abortion to receive chemo. She wished to have the baby, but the doctors did not give her that much time. The abortion broke her spirits. She died a few months later. I died, too. This isn't living. This is being numb until I die. I saw what drugs did to my mother.' He shook his head. 'Not for me. Whiskey, sex and mysteries about dead bodies are my drugs, and I hope they keep it all out of my mind.'

Part II

THEN

Chapter Ten

Evagoras was your typical Athenian. His roots were from everywhere but Athens, yet there he was. Stuck with thousands of his fellow townsfolk in the big metropolis's traffic, cursing the bad weather as he made his way home from the bank. He fixed his thick glasses upon his nose and focused on the large droplets of water that were diving out of the deep charcoal clouds roaming the autumn sky above. 'A light drizzle and they all drive like fucking snails. 'Come on,' he shouted as his horn joined in the cacophonic symphony of the miles-long gridlock.

With the help of soaking wet police wardens, the line of cars began to move once again. None received a single thank you. Athenians had had enough. They blamed everyone for the hopeless situation of their streets and wardens were a part of the system. A failed system.

Evagoras turned onto his street an entire hour after he clocked off work. His apartment was -according to distance- only fifteen minutes away from Attica Bank. 'Perfect!' Evagoras did sarcasm well. The drizzle had morphed into an aggressive downpour as he searched for a vacant parking spot near his block. None were to be found. 'I wish I had a house with a garage,' he whined. 'Yeah, keep playing the lottery. High chances of that happening!' His gelled up black hair was stuck to his face as he opened the building's front door, after a sprint in the rain. His wife, Stella, found him standing still by the door, panting.

'Not sure if I should make a joke about being forty and unfit or to shout about the bucket of water you are emptying on my dry clean floors.'

'How about a kiss and a wish that everything is going to work out? I'm tired.'

'Try being with your kids all day!' She approached and lay a gentle kiss on his lips while pushing back his renegade hair from before his sweet eyes. The boy she had once fallen in love with was still there, trapped inside this tired grown man.

'Where are the little monsters? It's way too quiet in here.'

'Finished their homework, ate all their food and rushed downstairs to their mates. Alexandro bought the new Playstation.'

'If I ever get a promotion like his dad...'

'Sssshh. Money isn't everything. Go have a hot shower and come have a quiet romantic meal with me.'

As Evagoras took off his brown jacket, he noticed the letter stuck into the frame of the hallway mirror. 'What's this?'

'It's a letter from your great aunt, Thalia.' Stella's voice came from the kitchen.

'About?'

'Didn't open it, dear. It's addressed to you.'

Evagoras tore the letter open with haste. Thalia was his

richest relative. His grandmother's youngest sister, Thalia never married but made a fortune from her sweet-making business during the seventies. *'Could she be dead? Am I in the will?'*

His eyes rushed along the one paragraph note. He trudged to the kitchen and stood in the doorway. Stella turned to see the enigmatic look that had settled upon his face. 'What does it say?'

'It is addressed to *dear relative*. Who writes that?'

'Your aunt was never fond of people. I doubt she knows all your names.'

'Yet she could name all her fifty-two cats and eight dogs!'

'Don't forget the parrots!'

Their laughter filled up the small compact kitchen.

'Well, go on. Read,' Stella urged him. 'I've restrained my inner curiosity since it was delivered.'

Evagoras coughed and brought the piece of elegant paper to eye level.

'Dear relative. I hope this letter finds you and yours well. I am unfortunately not in the best of spirits. I sense my end is near. Not complaining of course. I have lived my eighty-two years on this planet to the fullest. I know I must have seemed to you all as a distant witch (replaced the w with a b if you must) and maybe I was. I am not a people's person. I will not pretend to particularly know you. But after my last medical appointment (and death sentence delivered) my lawyer requested names for my will. The money will go to charity of course (no one needs that much cash), but the house, the cottage, a couple of apartments, stocks of the sweet business and land, can be yours. I am inviting all my close living so-called first-degree relatives to my mansion for the long weekend of October 28th coming up. Bring your identity cards and birth certificates. If you make it up here, you will make the will. Pun intended. Regards, Thalia.'

Stella let go of the wooden ladle and blew a renegade strike of hair from her slightly sweaty face. 'Well, well, well. She does love paragraphs, huh?'

'That's your comment?'

'What would you rather have me say? I've been married to you for fifteen years, mister. I know damn well that there is no chance we are not rushing to the island and being first in line to greet the old bat. If money is involved, Evagoras is involved.'

Evagoras chuckled and folded the letter. 'Get your mother on the phone. She is having the kids that weekend. I will book our tickets.'

On the morning of Saturday, the 26th, Evagoras and Stella stepped off the coach and laid foot in Igoumenitsa after a six hour drive from the capital. Evagoras had his eyes on his watch as the bus driver opened the bus's haul for his tired morning passengers to take their luggage.

'What time is it?' Stella asked as she placed her red sunglasses upon her thin nose and gazed out at the small seaside town that nested comfortably in the bay. The dark blue waters carried various ships upon their waves.

'The ferry departs in half an hour,' Evagoras replied knowing exactly what his wife meant with her question. 'We could walk down but I believe my wife wishes for a taxi.' After a decade of being wed, couples either drift apart or turn into a single thinking entity.

'Praise the Lord.'

The ferry set off on time that fine morning. A few

autumn clouds were scattered on the turquoise blanket that roofed Greece, but none seemed menacing enough to carry rain. Stella stood on the open-air terrace that ran around the ferry's bridge and let her black hair loose in the wind. The saltiness of the Ionian crept up her nostrils. 'Screw you, foggy Athens,' she joked. 'I hope we get the island house.'

No reply came from her usually chatty husband. '*He must be eating*,' she thought and held back a giggle upon the idea. She looked around her. Few passengers were out in the wind. Most sat inside for the short journey of an hour and a half. Less on calmer summer days. Evagoras stood meters away from her, gazing down to the lower deck. Stella smiled and snuck up behind him. She pinched his sides, whispering in his ear. 'Looking at women, mister?'

'Yes,' he answered quite absent-mindedly.

'Excuse me?' Her cheery tone shifted.

'Look.'

Stella turned her attention to the direction of his nod. A woman over forty sat dressed in all black on a green wooden bench staring at the sea. You could feel her sorrow. As if her pain had created its own personal aura of darkness and emptiness. She looked awfully pale and weak. 'Is that…'

'Has to be. My cousin, Moira.'

'What a tragedy.'

Evagoras nodded but then his face turned stern. 'Hope she doesn't use her story to get into the old lady's good books. All of the cousins that show up deserve an equal share.'

'Well said, dear.' Stella rested her head upon his broad shoulders, closed her eyes and focused her hearing upon the waves crushing against the boat. She imagined it could be the last time they would be so relaxed. They had to be on their best behavior in front of old Thalia. They were doing okay in life according to Stella. Middle class. Not poor, not rich, but she knew what kind of man she had married. Ambitious from the get-go. She knew well that money would make him a better person. A more relaxed, stress-free spouse. A happier entity. Evagoras needed a house, not an apartment. He needed vacations to Greek islands, European cities, and exotic destinations, not weekends at her grandma's village or day trips to the beach. He needed a better vehicle, not too flashy as he feared the 'bad-eye' but surely an upgrade on his Japanese old banger.

Little did she know that it would be the final time that she rested comfortably upon her husband. By the end of the weekend, she would be resting her head upon the chest of his dead body.

At port, Stella approached the woman in black. She needed to get a feel of her as she put it to her husband who snapped behind closed teeth. 'Don't you dare. You don't have to stir the pot every time you see.' But Stella already was holding the ladle and walking up to his cousin.

'Excuse me? Moira? It's you, right? Hi, I'm Stella, your cousin Evagoras' wife?'

The woman raised her head slowly, almost painfully. She looked like she was underfed and out of energy. She nodded and coughed. 'Yes, yes. I remember you. I'm guessing you are heading up to granny Thalia's mansion, huh?'

'Well, it was hardly a choice. The poor old thing. Alone at the very end. She needs us.'

'Better alone at the end, rather than taking others with you.'

Stella clenched her throat and her eyes rushed to focus elsewhere.

Evagoras's voice saved her from the awkwardness of the

long silence. 'Found a taxi, dear. Come on.' His voice journeyed over and gave her a chance to turn away from the face of complete sorrow opposite her. 'Hi, cousin Moira,' he continued, raising his voice and waving with his right hand as his left was used as a shade above his beady eyes.

'Come on, Stella,' Moira said, walking by her side. 'He has found us a taxi.'

The taxi driver was an obese woman in her fifties with black Rasta hair and eight earrings on each ear. She enjoyed having people in her cab that weren't from the island. That was the main reason that she normally lingered by the docks during the morning and the airport during the evening. But, alas, none of her three passengers seemed to be in a mood to utter a single word. Disappointed with the failure of her set of grilling questions, she dropped them off outside of the gates of the mansion on the hill. She had learnt nothing about them nor received any piece of information that was new to her. Her goal was to acquire knowledge daily, even if trivial.

The mansion's tall gate was shut.

'We will walk from here.' Evagoras took out his wallet. Moira exited the vehicle and approached the gate. 'Guess she isn't chipping it on the tab,' he whispered to his wife.

With the taxi rushing away back to the port, Stella pushed open the gate.

Evagoras, Stella and Moira walked up the hill to find more of their relatives outside of the house. Evagoras put on the face with which he welcomed rich customers at the bank. Took on the same tone as well. 'Uncle Paris! Cousin Sebastian! How are you? Alkione, you are looking radiant, my dear. I see Sebastian is treating you well.'

Pleasantries went back and forth, before Evagoras finally asked. 'Why are you three standing out here?'

'The door is locked.' Alkione pulled on the door handle and rang the doorbell as to prove her point. 'And no one is in,' the ginger-haired woman with the red thin-framed reading glasses added.

'Maybe she is out with a maid or a nurse? I doubt she lives here alone. She could not take care of this palace all by herself,' Stella said as she walked up to the row of windows that nested in the well-maintained and trimmed ivy. She peered inside. 'The curtains are drawn back, and it appears spotless inside.'

'Maybe we are too late.' Moira's weak voice was heard. The woman in black stood by a row of pots featuring an impressive array of cactuses.

'How early did she want us to be here?' Sebastian snapped.

A faint smile spread upon Moira's pale face. 'Always the bright one cousin. I meant she could have died last night, peacefully in her sleep. Dead without a will. All to the cats.' The notion settled in well. Their uncle Paris crossed himself and shook his head in disbelief. 'My poor aunt...'

'Shall we call the police? An ambulance?'

'And have them knock this fine wooden door down? No need. A woman like great-aunt Thalia doesn't bother opening the door for any help,' Moira said as she lifted pot by pot. 'Voila. An extra key.' Evagoras took the key from her raised hand. 'Bravo! Now, quick. Let's find her and hope she is okay.' The mansion's front door flung open as the eager six future beneficiaries entered.

'Spread out,' sixty-year-old Paris said as they all walked in as a pack, all taking in the wealth on display around them.

'Hello?' Sebastian called out as he rushed up the marble stairs.

Moira settled down on a tall-back burgundy leather armchair and gasped for air. The journey and the commotion proved too much for her system. She sat back and placed her hands upon her heart. Five people were enough to locate a corpse. She closed her eyes and exhaled with a sigh as she waited for news. News came but were not what she was expecting.

'The house is empty. Thalia is nowhere to be found,' Alkione informed her as she sat down on the sofa opposite her. 'What do we do now?'

'Wait for her to come home. She is probably at the market or at a friend's for coffee.'

'And you couldn't have suggested that first before implying that she is dead?'

'Death and I are well acquainted. He will come for us all one day.'

'Funny how slower time seems to move when you are bored out of your effin mind!' Uncle Paris stood in front of the large oval mirror that occupied the wall leading to the corridor from the main living room. He had his fingers on his face and was pulling back his relaxed facial skin. 'Bloody wrinkles. Can you believe I turned sixty this year?'

No reply came from his nieces and nephews who sat in the living room as a bunch of grounded moody teenagers.

'Can you believe I turned sixty this year?' He repeated his question louder. 'Me? Your youngest uncle this old!'

'You still look fabulous,' Stella commented and placed her hand upon her husband's as to stop him fidgeting. 'I remember when I first met you at our engagement party.

You were the most handsome man there. I remember asking Evagoras about you that night.'

'And what did my nephew had to say?'

Stella laughed. 'Oh, he told me, don't get your hopes up, my uncle's boyfriend will be here shortly.'

Paris released a roar of a laugh. 'Oh, dear Stella. You are too kind. Boyfriend, huh? Who was I dating at the time?' He tapped his jaw apparently lost in deep thought.

'The well-endowed fireman, if I recall correctly from all your bragging,' Sebastian said, as he stood up from the armchair and walked over to the window to check for the twentieth time if Thalia was walking up the pathway.

Paris snapped his fingers. 'Oh, yes! Nico, the flame. Ooooff. What a man! After our first time, I couldn't walk...'

'Too much info, uncle. Please!'

'Oh, Sebastian. Don't be such a prude.'

Alkione pushed her glasses down to the tip off her nose and squatted by the huge wooden bookcase. Her index finger instinctively ran down the scar in the wood on the side of the bookcase while her green eyes journeyed along the book titles housed upon the shelves. 'Interesting collection, our great-aunt has. From Lord of the Rings to Nietzsche to Shakespeare to Alki Zei.'

'I don't know what's worse. The agonizingly long wait or the mindless chatter we are trying to create?'

All eyes turned towards Moira. Many had formed a reply in their minds. A bitter reply. None though spoke. Tragedy, a Greek word, was not strong enough to describe the torment Moira had been through just months ago. Her family members opted for silence. Let the hurt wounded animal bark and bite as much as it pleases.

Evagoras stood up. 'I'm hungry. How about a scavenger's hunt into the kitchen kingdom?'

Stella smiled as he stared at her and stood up with him. Evagoras ground his teeth. No one had bothered to reply. 'Come on. It's nearly midday. We are Greek and Greeks eat.'

'I'm starving, cuz,' Sebastian spoke as he walked towards him, 'but what if it annoys auntie Thalia to come find us around her table eating away on her goods? Maybe she is indeed out grocery shopping for us?' he continued lowering his voice.

'Let's give it another half an hour, then.'

'And then what?' Alkione finally drew her attention away from the books. 'We have lunch and wait some more? Maybe it would be wise to contact someone?'

'Like the police?'

'Well, maybe not yet, uncle. But we could ask around the neighbors.'

Moira chuckled. 'She hated people. Can you imagine her hanging around with anyone from down the street? In those little houses? With their boring talk about house chores? Thalia is a wonder woman. A business mind like no other. Strong and opiniated.' Moira shook her head. 'I'm not pointlessly walking around socializing.'

Suddenly, a loud smashing sound made them jump.

'What the…?'

'It came from down the hallway.'

'The kitchen.'

The group moved as one. An arrow shape of humans travelling through the hall, and Evagoras was the point. 'Auntie Thalia?' he called out. 'Hello?'

Pieces of what was most definitely a vase rested on the floor in a small pool of water. The blue porcelain had no chance as it fell from the kitchen counter to the hard kitchen tiles. Three chrysanthemums lay together by the shattered ornament. The thin white curtains floated in the air.

'Must have been the wind,' Paris stated what he believed to be the obvious culprit.

'This breeze?' Moira stood by the open window, the curtains dancing carelessly around her. 'Probably not strong enough to blow out a candle on the counter.

'What is your suggestion then, Sherlock?'

'Without putting my hand on fire, stray cat.'

Everyone lowered their eyes and looked around. Everyone but Evagoras who had opened the fridge. His mouth opened as he witnessed the uncooked pastitsio in a large Pyrex sitting alone on the middle shelf. A row of ice-cold Mythos and Alpha beers rattled in the door. He whistled out loudly. 'Lunch and more! Heat up the oven, babe. And no Sebastian, we are not waiting any longer. This was made for us. She has been delayed or whatever. She could be on an airplane off to some meeting or whatever. She left this for us.'

'Or will be back to heat it herself shortly.'

'Or whatever,' Moira mimicked Evagoras's voice.

'Oh, bloody hell.' Paris took the dish out of the fridge and shoved into the oven. 'Switch it on, Stella. Too much talk is poor, my granny used to say. Just do it. And get those beers opened and served. What a day!'

Soon, the rich aroma billowed and invaded their nostrils, taunting their empty stomachs.

'Funny how a dish, a specific scent can trigger memories. I do believe this, and moussaka bring back fond memories to all Greeks. It marked our childhood. As hard as things were, families gathered and enjoyed a Sunday feast together. That's the core of our civilization.'

'And I thought that was democracy,' Alkione joked and

placed her hand on her uncle's shoulder. 'Well said, Paris. Indeed, those Sunday meals at grandma's were so much more than just food. They were the glue that bonded us with our parents and grandparents.'

'So, I guess poor rats like me aren't really Greek huh? No such Sundays for us...' Moira groused quietly as she walked off.

Evagoras and Sebastian exchanged a look and rolled their eyes. Both grabbed their cold beers as they sat around the kitchen table.

'Cheers, cousin!' Evagoras said, as he sighed while watching Moira drag her feet down the hallway. 'So, how's business?'

Sebastian continued drinking. He drank slowly and more than usual. He coughed as he lowered the bottle. 'Well, you know how things are at the moment. The imports weren't really worth it in the end.'

'So, what are you up to now?'

'Oh, a lot. Keeping busy. Keeping the cash flow going. Got a few things set up.' He drank some more, before adding, 'actually, as we have time until lunch is served, there is an amazing opportunity in travelling right now. Global Ventures. People are enjoying trotting around the globe and becoming millionaires as they do. This one guy, here in Greece, just bought a Ferrari with his earnings. I am just starting out and the income is excellent.'

'Tell me more,' Evagoras said as he raised his beer and nodded toward his relative. Uncle Paris came closer and sat down with them.

Stella shook her head slightly. 'Keep an eye on the food, please, Alkione,' she said and wondered off behind Moira.

Stella rubbed the back of her neck as she walked past the paintings in the hall. Acrylic landscapes forever trapped inside heavy frames. She looked behind her. *'Must be the breeze.'* She took a few more steps forward before stopping at an open door. Her eyes tried to focus into the darkness of the small room. *'What's that screeching?'*

'Moira?' she called out without stepping into the room.

'Yes?' Moira's reply came from the living room. Stella bit her lower lip and ran her hands through her hair. She closed the door and rushed down the hall.

'Hey Moira…'

The woman in black did not reply. She stood with her back to Stella, gazing out the window.

'I'm not even going to try to understand the pain you are going through. Only you know that burden. However, I have been told that I am a tremendously good listener. Such hardships should not nest inside us, eating us away like a tumor.'

'I have nothing to say. And nothing I do say will change the facts.'

'Life if for the living, Moira. You have to keep…'

'I have to do nothing. I owe no one shit.'

'The years go by quickly, my dear. Sooner or later, we will all meet again in Heaven. Our souls…'

Moira swung around. 'Oh, please. I don't believe in fairy tales. I am a grown up with a mind.'

'It's our religion. You husband is looking down at you, keeping an eye on you, your guardian angel…'

'And how exactly is he looking down at me? His eyes have been eaten by earthworms six feet under. There is no magic, Stella. Just make-believe to help simple minds get through the day. Our planet is not a reality show for ten billion floating-in-space souls. Yes, Agatha Christie is up there looking down watching us reading her books or watching the movies made from her stories. Nelson

Mandela is having a chat with my boring clueless grandfather about world peace as they watch the on-going wars.'

'It's not like that. They all look down on their loved ones.'

'And what loved ones does a soldier killed 2000 years ago still have today? What about babies that died before even turning one? They have no memory of any relatives…'

'You overthink things.'

'And even so, how creepy is it to believe that when you shower, sit on the toilet, have sex, pick your noise or whatever, that all your dead relatives are looking down upon you? This is not Neverland, Tinkerbell. This is real life.' Moira said the last words as she walked past Stella and headed outside. Stella placed her head between her hands and fell back into the armchair on her right.

'What a woman! Ooff.'

Minutes later, she heard her husband's voice as he looked for her. He found her in the exact spot she had comfortably rested since her talk with Moira. Her feet were swollen from the journey and her ankles were doing her no favors today. 'Missed me, my love?'

'That and the fact that food is ready. This wolf is starving.'

'Kids in slums in India are starving, babe. You are just hungry.'

He leaned forward and kissed her forehead. She grabbed onto him and raised herself up.

'Where's cousin Moira?'

'Outside.'

'Moira? Moira? Food!'

Moira walked in through the front door. 'Stop shouting like a peasant if you are planning on living in such a luxurious mansion.' She did not pause to hear any reply. With Moira out of sight, Evagoras pulled his wife closer and brought his lips near her ear. 'God, I hate that woman.'

'I doubt she believes in God.'

'Yeah, you're right. Only the Devil would have her.'

The couple shared a controlled laugh before heading back to the kitchen. Stella looked to her right. The doors to the rooms were all open again. 'Did you open these?'

Evagoras shook his head and continued down the hallway.

Alkione had set the table. The six sat around the table and with the tiny dab of guilt devoured by the mouth-watering pasta, the first bites began. If any guilt remained, it had vanished as night fall came and Aunt Thalia had not.

'We should call someone. There is no excuse for having waited so long. I'll call the hospital and you the police, Sebastian.'

Sebastian nodded to his uncle and took out his cell phone while Paris sat down to use the land line. Typical Greeks, both wandered about as they spoke, waving their arms. Both reported back to the group in a matter of minutes.

The wind howled outside as if it was king of the unprotected hill. It swirled around Thalia's numerous flowerpots and shook around her trees.

'Clouds are gathering.'

'News mentioned rain tomorrow.'

Evagoras rubbed his wife's back and smiled at her. 'Missing Thalia and all aside, it feels nice to be here with you without the kids. Some alone time without them interrupting us all the time.'

Stella looked at him sideways. She was thinking of something sweet for a reply though with the need to mention that their kids were not the monsters he often made them out to be. She opened her mouth but was not allowed to comment. Paris re-entered the room the only way he knew how. Theatrically. He placed one hand on his forehead and declared, 'thank the saints and all the prophets, in the hospital, she is not. Neither by name, nor anyone fitting her description.'

'Nothing from the police as well. I gave my number if anything come up. As it is night-time and she has not returned, they promised to send a unit to patrol around the village and near-by areas just in case she wandered off. Tomorrow, they advised me to fill in a missing person's report if we have no news by noon.'

'And that we should do,' Alkione said and stood up. 'Anyone for coffee? Some biscuits and such?'

Moira rolled her eyes with her back to the group that was complimenting Alkione on her kind gesture. All of course began ordering their beverages with instructions according to their taste.

'Moira? Coffee?'

'No, thank you, Alkione. I don't need to be served. I will make my own when I feel like it.'

Moira ignored the warnings of the wind and walked outside. The patio bench suited her just fine. The moon was the only company she needed. A silent companion to her lonely nights. Earth's lone satellite reminded Moira of something her Aunt Thalia had said about her deceased parents. On the day of their funeral, none the less. 'Your mum was like the moon. She appeared mystical and magical and shiny, but she had no light of her own. She was forced to forever be with her husband and journey around with him. She never set any goals for herself. She was a satellite of that brute. Oh, my poor sister could have lived a tremendous life, yet she got knocked-up and quickly married. Different times, you see. And for what? To have you and worry about you and your health until the day she died. I'm pretty sure she was pleased as their plane fell...'

'Bitch!' Moira had replied to her drunken aunt.

That was the last time she spoke to Thalia. And then so many years later, the letter came. A letter that found Moira in need.

Midnight found all six occupants still awake. Bathed, in their pyjamas and tucked in bed, yet still very much wide awake.

Alkione stood in front of the en-suite's mirror. She placed both hands on her face and pulled her skin back. *'Funny how such a silly move can remind you on how you used to look.'* She placed her index finger in her blue jar and raised its white cream to eye level. *'Do your magic.'* She rubbed it in, hating the feel of the bags under her eyes. *'Oh, you look amazing... for forty.'* She mimicked the latest casting director's voice. *'But the role is about a young lawyer just starting out. I'm sorry.'*

'I haven't had a decent role in years,' she exhaled.

'What was that, dear? You talking to me?' Sebastian's voice came from the bed. He had lit the two apple and cinnamon candles he had bought from IKEA -Alkione's favorites. He knew his wife was down after the latest rejection and he also knew well that dramatic actresses overreacted over everything. Also to his knowledge was the fact that she had not been intimate with him since her dismissal from the play she had her eyes set on. He lay on top of the bed, dressed only in his black designer boxer shorts. A gift from Alkione. She loved how his bulge looked in them.

'Nothing, babe. Just muttering to myself,' she replied. 'Tired from acting polite all day. Even the best actresses can't stay in character all the time. I'm not *that* method,' she continued as she walked into the room. Her eyes fell upon the candles as her nose recognized the aromatic scent floating in the air. Her pupils quickly moved away from the flames and focused on her nearly naked spouse.

'I see you are in your hotel mood.'

Sebastian patted the bed. 'Come, let me get you in the mood, too.'

'I see from the look in your eyes that I shouldn't even bother with the long day, traveling, headache routine.'

'Nope.'

Alkione giggled. 'We are not in the will yet. You have that celebration thing going on.'

'My celebration thing?'

'You know. When one of your silly schemes works out and delivers a profit.'

Sebastian sat up. 'Silly schemes? Those silly schemes support us…'

'Enough until my next gig.'

Sebastian looked down at his feet. 'I see you're in your arguing mood after pretending to be happy all day.'

'Fuck you, Bastian.'

'Well, that was what I was hoping for,' he said as he waved his hands around.

Alkione sighed. 'Okay, let's not kill this again. We are both failures. Two forty-plus year olds without a penny to their names and we need this inheritance. We will get it. Now, no more talk. Let's watch some goofy videos on your phone to relax for a while and then I'll take those sexy boxers off you.'

'Sounds like a deal.' Sebastian chuckled. He opened his mouth to speak again but opted not to comment. It would have slaughtered the mood. *'Lucky, we don't have kids. We would go bankrupt.'*

In the room by theirs, Moira sat with a hot mug in her hands. She gazed out the window into the dark horizon. Her eyes travelled with a lone grey cloud as it ventured alone in the night sky, blocking the starlight. She brought her coffee to her lips and took a small sip. Her chest moved up and down as she clenched her jaw. 'Screw you, God! There! I said it!' Her watery eyes let single drops to slither down her cold cheeks. She opened the top drawer of the antique bedside table with the meticulously carved markings and took out her pill box. All the different colors and shapes were organized by the day and separated into morning, midday, and night. She took all four in one go and washed them down with a big gulp from her beverage.

A loud bang from behind, made her jump. Her mug fell to the floor and shattered before her eyes, dumping onto the white rug. Moira turned around and gasped. No one was there, but the cross nailed to wall was hanging upside down. Moira placed her hand upon her maniacally beating heart. 'Jesus!'

Even Moira could see the irony in that. She took slow small steps towards the religious artifact. She examined its nails. One was loose. *'Someone must have slammed a door…'*

In the next bedroom, Paris was oblivious to any banging. He sat on the toilet naked with his headphones on. As always, when in-between relationships, he was googling porn. Minutes later, he exited the bathroom, checked that all the window shutters were closed, and that the door was locked. He smiled and let his bath towel fall to the ground. He leaped onto the bed and pressed play. His hands were soon caressing his erection. He switched off the lights and let himself get lost in his cowboy fantasy. Suddenly, the lights came back to life. With eyes wide open, Paris sat up and looked around. One switch was above his head, the other by the door. 'What the...' He paused his video and removed his prized headphones. He kept his eyes on the door as his hand reached for the switch above his head. Darkness returned to the room. He waited. Minutes passed and the darkness remained. He made himself comfortable again and pressed play. He kept the headphones off. Soon, he continued with his masturbation. As soon as he placed his headphones back on his ears, the lights switched back on.

'For fuck's sake!' Paris always swore when nervous. He flung his phone to the side, picked up his towel as to cover himself and rushed to the door. He pulled down the handle. It was locked. Paris placed his back to the wall. 'Hello? Who's there? This isn't funny!'

The room stood before him empty. He took steady steps forward while his eyes swam side-to-side. He approached the bathroom door and pushed it open with his leg. From a good meter away, he looked inside the small room. He was alone. The tapping on the window made him jump. 'I'm gonna have a heart attack tonight!' he said as he noticed the tree branch being pushed against the glass by the strong wind.

The last bedroom on the right, also had tenants that were wide awake. Evagoras pushed open the last window and leaned outside with his cigarette.

'Dear, you're freezing me.'

Evagoras sucked in as much smoke as he could in two

long puffs and flicked his lit bud out into the gust passing by the mansion. He quickly closed the window and turned his attention to his wife who had snuggled under the violet duvet. 'It's not that cold. It's still autumn.'

'Up here it's colder. And the wind carried that sharp freeze attack of the sea.'

'Sharp what attack?' Evagoras chuckled and began to undress. 'My turn for a shower. Hot water, ok?'

'Thought it wasn't cold.'

'Still want a nice hot shower after this day.'

'Hotter than ours and better pressure.'

'Nice to own a mansion, huh?' he said as he sat down on the bed to pull off his socks. He felt both sticking to his tired feet.

'If we do get it, we're not keeping it though. We are definitely selling it, right? We need the cash...' Stella paused. She was used to her hot-headed husband interrupting her by now. 'We are selling it, right?'

Evagoras shook his head and stood up. He pulled down his jeans as to avoid eye contact. 'Well, if we get stocks or another piece of land, we could make money of that and make this our home.'

'Home?' Stella felt the yell journey up her throat and fly out towards him. She sat up straight. Her eyebrows moved closer together. 'Now, listen here, mister. Our hometown is Athens. You aren't moving me to a small island...'

'Corfu is one of the largest...'

'And you are definitely not dragging the kids out of their schools and away from their friends. Big houses have big problems and big expenses. Cleaning and fixing and such. No way, senor. We sell it and with the cash we live a better life in Athens and we can holiday on a different island every summer.'

Evagoras released a heavy sigh and with his head down, he walked towards the en-suite's door. 'As always, you're probably right, dear. Money will free us. No more worrying about the kids, their futures and their studies. We will be able to offer them a good life.'

'And God knows they deserve to see stress-free parents. I feel we owe them more of our time.'

Evagoras nodded, blew her a kiss and closed the bathroom door behind him.

Stella was also right about the water. It fell hot and with strength. Liberating, cathartic, therapeutic. Evagoras needed it. He rubbed the lavender-scented shower gel into his aching muscles. He let his mind go hollow, blank. He could not think of a future where he was not rich. If only they knew where Thalia had drifted off to. By the time he exited the bathroom along with a huge steam cloud, Stella had also drifted away into dreamland. He quickly dried himself off and naked as he was, he carefully made his way to his wife. He settled by her side, spooning her in his embrace. Soon, he was fast asleep, caressed by the warmth of her body and serenaded by the lullaby of her gentle breathing.

Chapter Eleven

The sun crept out of the Ionian sea and shot its hot rays upon the shrimp-shaped island. It reminded the six occupants of the mansion of summery days when even a thin t-shirt was a piece of clothing too much. Besides an overthrown clay pot featuring a small decaying cactus, nothing betrayed the wind's behavior the night before.

Moira covered her entire body in black, nevertheless. She could hear the humans she shared the house -and DNA- with, exchanging wishes for a good morning and an even better day in the hallway. She mimicked vomiting, smiled at her evil ways, and opened the curtains to gaze outside. She was in no mood to socialize more with any of them. She decided on remaining in her room until they had all finished their breakfast. 'Like locusts in Thalia's Garden. Eat away,' she whispered as she took a book borrowed from the living room into her hands. She had always wanted to read Anne Frank's diary. She was not sure why. Because it was famous, because it contained a story of suffering and loss or maybe because the holocaust and its pain amazed her in a horrific kind of way? It truly puzzled her. She knew her own agony well. Was others' torment making her feel better such a bad thing? Moira was not so sure. She could feel the transformation inside her. She was never what most would call a happy person. Her health did not let her embrace such emotions often. But now, she found herself angry, sad, and bitter. A dangerous combination. Especially for a single mother that had two kids she knew she had to think of but did not have the strength for. 'Money would make it easier with the chore of raising them. And I deserve the best care...' she muttered and opened the translated work to page one.

Below, Paris was clapping at the sight of fresh toast popping out of Thalia's orange designer toaster that dominated the corner under the cupboards. 'Mmmm, what a divine smell. This bread is home made for sure.'

'I can't imagine Thalia baking to be honest.'

Paris turned towards Alkione. 'Home made by a local. Someone like Thalia buys her way through life.'

'Sounds so easy.' With each word, the ironic smirk on her face grew.

'Watch it, dear. Jealousy is picking through. We don't wish for our true colors to shine through, huh?'

'Any news from the police, cuz?' Sebastian asked Evagoras, shutting down their conversation.

'Nada. I think after breakfast, we should head down to the station.'

'Thought they said noon.'

Evagoras opened a jar of strawberry jam and before dipping in his knife, said, 'What's the point in waiting?'

Sebastian shrugged his shoulders and bit into his chunk of cheddar cheese.

'I was thinking,' Paris said as he sat down by his nephews. 'Could she have mixed up the days? She could be arriving back home today. That is why the house was so clean, the kitchen stocked up and the beds ready for us. Thalia probably has a local lady take care of such affairs. I'm sure it is a simple matter.'

'Then why has her cell phone been off since yesterday?'

Paris smiled at Stella. 'When was the last time anyone of us spoke to her? Years? Who is to say she still has the same number?'

'Uncle Sherlock!' Sebastian said and his screeching laughter escaped his large front teeth.

'Okay, okay...' Evagoras sighed. 'We will wait until noon. But no longer than that.' He raised his coffee, saluted his relatives, and took his first sip rather loudly. Stella shook her head and thought how she would be mortified if she had to sit next to him at any formal event and be served soup.

'Wanna hear a joke? I heard a good one the other day.'

'Go on, uncle.'

'What's the difference between a pregnant lady and a lightbulb?'

He let a few seconds pass, watching their puzzled faces, before heading to the punch line.

'You can't unscrew a pregnant lady!'

Their laughs reached Moira's ears. She was forced to read the same line from her book three times. She ground her teeth and gazed outside. The horizon always had a magical way of calming her. That thin line where earth and sky met. Yet nature was one. 'Two sides to us all,' she whispered. She rubbed her eyes with her palms. She felt drowsy, having taken her pills on an empty stomach. Her thumbs ran circles on her temples as she coughed. 'Maybe if I wasn't so damn sick, my good side would be in the driver's seat more often.' She stood up and with small steps, decided to head down to the kitchen in hope that the 'annoying five' would be leaving the it shortly.

Not much natural light managed to reach the corridor outside of the guest rooms. Moira ran her hand along the planks of wood that decorated the walls. 'What's the point? Just paint the walls...' She knocked against the wood and listened to the sound. 'Weird rich folks. Just makes the hall darker and you lose space...'

Moira was pretty much still talking to herself when she finally reached the kitchen, breathless and with aching ankles. She smiled as she heard the men stepping outside for a smoke. She paused and waited. She placed her back against the wall and exhaled. 'Breath in through the nose, out from the mouth,' she repeated a doctor's advice to her as a child. 'It will help when your chest feels heavy,' he had said. Suddenly, she shivered. The hairs on the back of her neck stood at attention and made her twitch. She looked around her. She was alone between the tripod side table housing a Chinese vase with fake flowers of paradise and the tall ground light that looked like it had escaped Pixar's studios. She waited to hear the kitchen's door to the garden close before joining Stella and Alkione. *'Greek ladies and their freaking duties!'* Both women were gathering their husbands' and uncle's plates.

Stella caught a glimpse of the figure standing in the doorway. 'Oh, good morning, Moira.' She placed the dish with the cut cheeses back on the table. 'Come, have breakfast. Fancy a coffee?'

'Yes, why not? Thanks. Black, please.' Moira let her nice side speak. She had no strength in her body and her stomach was craving something more than strong pills. She sat down and grabbed a piece of bread. She spread out butter all sloppy on it and then dipped it in the pool of honey that she had poured onto her plate. A few bites later and she was feeling better already. Color had returned to her cheeks as Stella placed her coffee in front of her. The smoky white lines journeyed up. The rich aroma tickled her nostrils. She managed to thank her cousin's wife once again. She enjoyed her coffee in small sips while avoiding taking part in the small talk between the two women cleaning up the kitchen.

Outside, Evagoras had left the company of three and began to wander around the property that he hoped would one day -soon- be his. With his hands in his pockets, he gently whistled as he went along the brick path, inspecting the state of the building. A half smile appeared across his face. A grin that was always born from content. The building was well-maintained. Evagoras was in no position to afford or oversee a renovation of an estate, especially one this grand. As he stopped to smell a yellow rose, he heard it. A peculiar sound. Like knives grating against each other. Memories of his butcher father came flowing back. He stood up straight and took a few small steps forward. The noise turned into a chopping one. It maintained a rhythm. It was coming from around the corner.

'*A gardener?*' he thought as he took a few side steps to get a better view. 'Hello?' The sound abruptly stopped. 'Hello? Who is there? I am Evagoras…'

No one replied, but he heard footsteps. Their sound faded quickly. Evagoras ran around the corner. He caught a glimpse of a figure disappearing into the shadows provided by the oddly-shaped house. 'Hello? No need to run. I am a relative of Thalia's. She invited us up here,' Evagoras continued calling out as he chased the person. To his surprise, the shadows lead to a brick wall. 'What the...?' He placed his hands upon the wall. 'How can...?

Evagoras was still examining the wall when he felt the blade on his neck. He froze on the spot. The blade pressed against his neck's pumping artery. 'Please, I... I am a relative of Thalia's...'

'How do you know my name?'

The blade withdrew from his throat, cutting it slightly. Evagoras did not even quaver. He had suffered worst papercuts than this. He took a long step forward and turned around. A tall woman wearing a dirty purple dress stood before him. Her hair was tangled up and she was barefoot. Her emerald eyes stood out due to her sickly-looking pale skin. He would recognize those eyes anywhere.

'Auntie Thalia? It's me! Evagoras.'

'Don't talk to me, thief!' She waved her hedge shears at him. 'How do you know my name? Calling me auntie and shit! Stay back! Stay back I say!'

Evagoras placed his palms out front. 'I am no thief. I am not here to hurt you. You invited us here...'

'Us? There's more of you?' Her eyes opened wide as she frantically looked around her. 'What do you people want? Money?'

Evagoras controlled a smirk from being born. The honest answer to that would have been a powerful yes. 'We are your family. We have come to see you...' Evagoras dared to step closer.

Thalia's eyes moved around quicker than the shears in her hands. She screamed at the top of her lungs. 'Arggh! Help! Help! Somebody, help me.'

Evagoras jumped back, looking around. The emotion he felt was not one he would have expected at such a moment. It was not fright for himself or pity for his clearly delusional great aunt. It was embarrassment. *'Don't be foolish. No one knows you here anyway!'*

Thalia's yells were not strong enough to journey across her vast property and down the hill to her closest neighbors. They did though have enough might to reach the kitchen. The men arrived at the scene first, while the three ladies followed. All five stood in amazement at the sight of Thalia waving her garden shears at Evagoras who stood with his back against the wall.

'Your accomplices, thief? Why you dirty rascals, they should hang the lot of you...'

'Thalia, my dear. It's me. Paris.'

There was a change in Thalia's eyes. Like a light had been switched on behind them. Her clenched neck muscles relaxed, and her facial features settled back to their norm. Even clearly tired, aggravated, and ashen without a sign of makeup, Thalia was a true Greek beauty of a classy, aristocratic era long gone. 'Paris?' She lowered her garden tool and took a step closer. 'You're my cousin,' she said in almost a whisper.

'Yes, my dear. It's me. And that poor boy over there is Katie's boy. Evagoras. Your late sister's only son.'

'Late?' Thalia's voice came out broken. Her fingers twitched around in her shaking palms. She turned to face Evagoras again. She examined his face. 'You have her eyes.' She dropped the shears to the grass. 'Is my poor sister really dead?'

'Yes, auntie. You came to the funeral years ago, remember?'

'My memories elude me, child. My mind has not been kind to me lately.' She raised her hand. 'Come closer. I'm sorry, Evagoras.' She opened her embrace and welcomed him in. 'Paris,' she then said and kissed her cousin on both his cheeks. 'You look like my cousin, Gianni. Let me guess. You're little Sebastian.'

Sebastian straightened and approached her with arms wide open, gloating in the fact that his great aunt remembered him. 'Auntie.' Kisses were exchanged, before Thalia turned her attention to the group of women by the brick wall.

'And you lot are? The wives? Come out to the sun, let me get a better look. My eyes aren't what they used to be, either.'

'I'm Stella, Evagoras's wife.'

'Oh, yes, dear. I remember you from your wedding day. Dazzling you were and dazzling you managed to stay. Greek women don't age, do we?' Thalia let out a croaky laughter.

'And I am Alkione…'

'The actress that seduced Sebastian. Oh, I remember the gossip now. Welcome to my home, sweetie.'

Alkione stood motionless as the old lady kissed her. With her eyes wide open, she searched for her husband's gaze. 'Just kiss her back,' he mouthed.

Thalia let her go and raised her index finger at Moira. 'And whose kid are you?'

'Alice's daughter. Your sister…'

'Yes, I know who Alice is!'

'*Could have fooled me.*'

'Dead as well, right?'

Moira ground her teeth. She forced herself to a slight nod. '*Be polite. You need her money.*'

A few leaves danced around them as a gust of wind pushed them along.

'Let's get you inside, my dear.' Paris wrapped his arm around Thalia's shoulders. 'Where have you been? We have been looking for you since yesterday!'

'Oh, that's right. I invited you all up here, right?' Thalia asked as she walked with Paris down the path towards the kitchen door. 'Lawyer said to sort out my will. And I did four different ones!'

Thalia was the only one chuckling as they entered the house. 'Mmm, coffee,' Thalia said as she sniffed the air. 'Which one of you ladies will be as kind as to brew me one? Semi-sweet, please.'

Moira shook her head and controlled her tongue, as Stella and Alkione both pushed by her and rushed to fulfil their future benefactor's request.

'I'll take it in the living room, thank you. And some biscuits. I am terribly starved.'

'Maybe some toast and some eggs, then auntie?'

Thalia waved her palm. 'No, no, Evagoras. Coffee and biscuits will be fine for now.'

The three men followed her down the hall to the brightness by the daylight living room. 'You haven't eaten since yesterday? Where were you? We didn't see you and we walked all around the house.'

'I don't worry about food. Anyway, we are all together now and I am glad you are here. Only you showed up?'

The three men stared at her as she sat down by the fireplace. They exchanged worried looks. Neither had thought that she could have had invited more.

'Who? We are the closest!' Sebastian mouthed.

Thalia whistling made them turn their attention back to her. Suddenly, two cats, a fluffy light grey Persian and a slim beige Siamese, appeared from the hallway. Both walked along the carpet, with one eye fixed on the guests, and leaped onto Thalia's lap. Their purring filled the room as their rubbed their heads against her before settling down by her side.

'And they say you can't train cats. Maybe because most do silly noises at them. Just whistle. Works with dogs and they are so obedient, right?'

Paris looked at the cats with a puzzled gaze. 'Where were the cats?'

Thalia did not reply. She was busy stroking their heads and asking them if they were cold. She picked up a black remote control and aimed it at the fireplace. 'Voila!'

Flames came to life behind the protective glass. 'Latest tech. Pretty neat, huh?' Thalia asked sounding youthful.

'Wow. Is it real fire?' Sebastian asked, coming closer, placing his palms on the glass.

'Of course, it is, foolish child. Works with gas. Saves you the whole fuss with pieces of wood.'

'I'm almost forty, auntie. Not really a child anymore.'

'What? And what would that make me? One hundred? Time truly does fly!'

Just then, the two ladies walked in. One carrying the coffee and the other a small plate of an array of various flavoured biscuits. Moira had suggested a tray, but that way meant only one would get to serve Thalia.

Thalia paid no attention to them as they placed what they were carrying on the tripod table by her side. Her eyes never left Sebastian. 'Forty, almost. So, how many kids do you have?'

Sebastian swallowed a lump in his throat. He knew the Greek mentality well. Few things mattered to most and they formed a very short list. Religion, country, family. The fact that Evagoras had two children, gave him a major advantage to the inheritance. 'No kids, auntie.'

'You shoot blanks or is the wife sterile?' Thalia turned around and faced Alkione.

'Err, no. We made a choice not to have kids and to focus on our...' Alkione began to reply.

'Careers? He's always unemployed and I have never seen you on TV. To not have kids for such a reason is quite frankly a sin.'

'I am a theatrical actress. To not do television is a choice.'

'Yes, of the directors, not yours.'

Alkione's eyes watered up. 'I am not unemployed,' Sebastian spoke to pull the heat off his wife. 'I am involved in many businesses. I am an entrepreneur. Always looking for new ideas. You should be proud of us, auntie. We follow in your successful footsteps. You didn't bear children and you focused on your business...'

'Silence, child. I could not have children. Hostile uterus. What a term! I wish I could and you!' Her eyes went back to Alkione. 'To throw away such a blessing. And for what? This fool who believes himself as a businessman? If you were successful, you would not be here!'

'Now, auntie. I love and respect you, but you have no right insulting my wife...'

'Mmm, great coffee. And, oh, my favorite biscuits! How on earth did you know?' Thalia interrupted him and dipped a round biscuit into her hot beverage. 'Lovely house!' Her eyes ventured around the room. 'Whose house is this?'

'Excuse me?'

'Oh, sorry, Gianni. I forgot you were talking. Go on.'

'I'm Sebastian. Gianni's son.'

Thalia looked lost for words. Her hands began to tremble as she took a bite out of her soggy chocolate biscuit. 'Sebastian? Oh, yes, yes. If you say so. And I am Thalia. Thank you for having me. Maybe it's time that I went home. I've been here for hours. Armenian visit!' Thalia placed her hands on the arms of the chair as to push herself up.

'Sit, auntie,' Evagoras said, rushing to her side. 'This is your house. Look, it's your cats. What are they called? They are absolutely lovely.'

Moira rolled her eyes and walked over to the window. She passed behind Sebastian and whispered to his ear. 'And just like that, poof, you are out of the race.' Sebastian turned red and clenched his hands but did not reply.

'My cats? Yes, yes. You are right, my sweet boy. This is Arash and this fussy one is Anurak.'

'Interesting choices,' Stella said and came closer.

'I wanted names from their respective countries of origin. Anurak means angel in Thai, doesn't it my thin boy, hmm?' She spoke to the cat and stroked him all over, much to the feline's pleasure.

'And what does Arash mean?' Paris asked, trying to enter the conversation.

'Beats me. He was a gardener I once had here. He was from Tehran.'

'What happened to your other…?' Evagoras began to ask, but his wife cut him off and rephrased his question in a more elegant manner. 'Only the two pets, auntie? You were always a great animal lover. I remember the day we were introduced, and I was immediately fond of you because you spoke about your pets and your charity causes.'

'Just the two cats left. A bit hard at my age to look after more and I don't want any permanent help living here.' She took another sip and then dropped the bomb. 'Ever since I knew I was dying, I stopped collecting strays and found homes for my young ones. But these two old boys will stick with me until the end. Do you have children, Evagoras?'

'Oh, yes, auntie. Two boys.' He quickly pulled out his

phone and began to scroll for pictures. 'Here. See here. This is them at a trip to the Parthenon.'

'Lovely. Handsome young fellows. Must be hard raising children in this current economical crisis. A lot of money involved.'

'Well, yes. Stella and I both work, but of course any extra help would be a blessing in these harsh days.'

Thalia nodded in agreement and dipped another biscuit into her cup.

Paris found the opportunity to get back into the conversation. 'Harsh for us all. It is in times like these that we realize how important family is and that only your family will stick by you and support you. It is in these times that we need to share our belongings and...'

'And who are you dear? You speak funny. You in theatre or something? Why are you here alone? Where is your wife?'

Evagoras bit his bottom lip to imprison a raging laugh.

'Thalia! It's me! Paris!'

Thalia nodded. 'I remember! The one my mother called the sodomite!'

'Times have changed, dear. I am homosexual. Being gay is normal nowadays.'

'Please.' Thalia waved her hand. 'You can be straight and a sodomite. She called you that because you let every Tom, Dick and Harry hump the hell out of you.'

'Now, listen here you old hag...'

There was a loud gasp from the rest of the members of the family. Even Moira turned around with eyes wide open.

'What? It's not like she will remember it. Fuck you, Thalia. I am not a crawling dog like Evagoras. You were never a nice person and your whore of a mother was worst. Screw you and your money. I'm better off without it.'

A smile spread out on Thalia's face. 'Greek men and their proudness. The door is there, fool.'

Everyone remained silent as Paris stormed upstairs and began to loudly pack his things. Thalia continued with her biscuit feast.

The loud slamming of the front door broke the silence. Thalia finally raised her eyes from her empty cup. 'Don't you carry the pride of the Greek male, Sebastian? Shouldn't your lazy ass and your lazy wife be walking out that door, too?'

Sebastian's jaw dropped and he took a step closer to his great-aunt. 'But, auntie, you have got us all wrong. We are good people and...'

Alkione pulled him by his arm. 'I'm leaving,' she said and proceeded upstairs in a slow walk with her head held high and her gaze fixated on the Apollo statue in the corner of the top floor.

'Shame for a grown man to beg. Listen to your wife and off you go, freeloader.'

Soon, a second slamming of the front door echoed through the mansion.

'My poor door,' Thalia whispered. 'And then there were three.'

Moira remained the entire time in the armchair by the oval window and kept her gaze out of the room. Corfu might be famous for the beauty of its beaches and its crystal-clear waters, but its meadows and country villages carried a special charm of their own. The richness of colours provided by the wildflowers overtaking the deep green grass caught Moira's attention and she used them as a distraction to keep her mind out of the on-going commotion. She thought she was the least favorite to inherit the place as her 'sucking-up' skills were as bad as her social skills. She remained quiet. She had no plans of being kicked out alongside her relatives. After the second slamming of the door, she turned her body towards the room. The smirking faces of Stella and Evagoras annoyed her, yet her expression revealed no such emotion. *'They feel so sure of themselves!'* She knew she had to be very careful. She had to play her cards right and earn a place in the will. With the others gone, half of the fortune could easily be hers. She forced a smile and stood up. Thalia had finished off the last of the biscuits and her cup sat empty. Moira approached, picked up the tray and began to walk out of the room. 'Need anything else from the kitchen, auntie?'

'Oh, so it's auntie, now, is it? Thought it was bitch.'

The tray started to wobble in her hands. Moira quickly set it down on top of the country cabinet to her left. 'You remember that from twenty years ago?'

'Why would I forget? It was my sister's funeral. I was upset and you…'

'I was a twenty-year-old that had just lost both her parents. You think I was not upset as well? Do you really blame me? I know you never liked my father, but it was all just a tragic accident that cost us both, dearly.' Moira fought to keep her voice calm. She took a few steps forward and knelt by Thalia. *'Oscar winning time, baby!'*

'Tragic accidents seem to chase me, auntie. I wish I had my mother, your sister, with me. I… I lost my husband and my youngest child in a car accident.' Moira looked straight into Thalia's eyes. 'Can you imagine the pain? You know what a child means. It was always a dream of yours and God blessed me with three. He took one back, but I still have my other two. A boy and a girl. Oh, auntie, you would love them. They took after my mother. Looks and brains.'

Thalia smiled and placed her hand upon Moira's.

'I am a sick woman,' Moira continued. 'The medical bills are high, and I work as much as my health will allow me to but raising children alone does not come cheap. All I ask, is for a better tomorrow for my children. Your beloved sister's grandchildren. If you dislike me, that's fine. I hate me most of the time. Keep me out of your will but put my kids in it. Give them a proper home, maybe? Lord knows, they deserve a chance.'

Thalia leaned forward and brought her lips an inch away from Moira's ear. Moira could feel her hot breath as she whispered.

'God blessed me! Lord knows,' she mimicked Moira's slow, almost strained way of talked. 'Screw you, God. Isn't that what you said, blasphemer? You think I would give my hard-earned fortune to a sicko that curses the Lord?'

Moira opened her eyes wide and tilted her head.

'What? How…?'

Thalia's blank stare returned. 'I think its time I get going. I've been sitting here for hours. Time to go home and get some work done.'

Evagoras rushed to her side and quickly began explaining where they were.

'What's up, my boy? You look ashen. What's worrying you?'

'The fact that you are going to give this crying weakling half of what can be easily mine!' Evagoras whispered to his wife, but Moira's ear was a trained one. Moira stood up, took the tray, and rushed to the kitchen to look for some decent alcohol. A fine dry white made in Thessalia was just what she needed. She took the bottle upstairs with her. She only had half an hour to down the contents of the entire bottle as to give herself breathing space before the next round of pills that she had to swallow. Then, it was time to think. Time for a plan.

Chapter Twelve

The sun vanished quicker from the horizon as October was coming to an end. Long gone were the summer days when light freely roamed Greece until nearly nine o' clock. Now, it was not even seven and Moira watched as the last orange rays hid behind the wild domed hills to the West. There was a knock on her door.

'Moira?' Stella's voice was heard as she pushed open the door halfway. She waited for Moira to speak, before popping her head inside. 'You hungry, dear? With Thalia coming and going, we kind of forgot about dinner. Evagoras is going to order form a kebab house for the four of us. We are getting their variety boxes. A little bit of everything. Do you want something specific? Anything you don't eat?'

'Whatever you bring is fine by me.'

Stella nodded and her mouth opened as if she wanted to say something, but she did not. She closed the door behind her, and Moira heard her footsteps echo from the staircase.

The doorbell that was heard forty minutes later was Moira's signal to head downstairs. Her only goal was to not come into any sort of confrontation with her aunt. At least, not in front of Evagoras and Stella. They had to think that she was still in the race, or her plan would surely fail.

The large dining room filled up on the rich aroma of freshly well-cooked meat as Evagoras placed the packets of goods in the middle of the table, between the pitcher of water and the vase featuring flowers cut from the garden that evening by Stella.

The party of four ate mostly in silence but their body language was deafening. Tension and worry arose from the married couple who gazed upon Moira as a threat to their future as upper-class rich folk. Moira kept her eyes focused on her meal as her thoughts were driving her crazy. She scratched her arm awkwardly nearly after every other bite. Thalia on the other hand, had her gaze all over the place. She devoured her meal with her eyes traveling from one relative to the next. She seemed in high spirits. Her color had returned to her high-bone cheeks and she had fixed up her hair.

Wishes for a good night were exchanged on the way up after Stella and Moira had taken the dirty dishes back to the kitchen. Thalia had told them not to bother with the washing up as her cleaning lady would be in, in the morning.

'That bitch better not cost us our future!'

'Shh, Evagoras!' his wife said in a whispery manner, quickly closing the door behind her and locking it out of worry.

'We are so close! So, freaking close, Stella!'

'Exactly why you need to calm down. If Thalia hears

you and judges you the wrong way, we are out. This house freaks me out a bit. I feel like… never mind. It's just nerves and being away from home.'

'Like what?'

'Like we are not alone. Like back at our apartment when you know others are around. That sort of feeling.' Stella sighed and sat on the bed. 'And believe it or not, I miss the kids and the noise,' she added and sat down on the bed. Evagoras kicked off his trainers and climbed on the bed behind her. He sat on his knees and began to rub her back. 'Relax, dear. Enjoy a nice hot shower and let's hope for the best.'

'That's the spirit.' She turned her neck and kiss her husband. 'And even half a fortune is better than no fortune at all!'

'Even though we deserve it.'

'Moira needs money as well. She is your cousin after all.'

Evagoras sunk his upper teeth into his bottom lip. 'That one is off, you know?'

'If I went through everything she has been through, I doubt that I wouldn't be a bit off, too.' And with that said, she followed her husband's advice and headed to the bathroom for a long steamy shower. Minutes later, as the cleansing water soothed her body and the strong flowery fragrance of her shower gel took over her senses, Stella began to sing old favorite ballads from the time she was a carefree schoolgirl.

Her vocal abilities and the water coming out at high power covered the sound of the loud thud outside.

Stella stepped out of the bathroom feeling refreshed and full of energy. 'Babes, how about we watch some funny videos on your phone? Relax like we used to…'

An empty room welcomed her. 'Evagoras?' She looked around. *'Where did he go?'* She walked over to the door, shivering. A cold breeze had invaded the room. She pulled down the handle to peek into the hallway and the door was locked. From the inside. With her eyes fixed on the key, her heartbeats accelerated. She turned around. 'Evagoras?' she raised her voice. The room was cold. She turned her attention to the open window and placed her hand upon her heart. She rushed to look outside. Her screams echoed down the hill. Down below on the grass, lay her motionless husband, his legs twisted, and his arms spread out. She dropped her towel to the floor, wrapped her robe around her and in tears, she rushed outside. As she unlocked the door and exited to the hallway, the door to her right opened. Moira stepped out of her room. 'I heard you scream, what's wrong?'

Stella did not stop. 'It's Evagoras. He fell out the window. He is hurt.'

'I'm calling 112,' Moira said and followed Stella down the stairs, with her phone in hand.

Stella ran to her husband, yelling out his name. He did not reply nor flinch. 'God, no, please,' a tearful Stella said sobbing as she placed her head upon his chest. 'Don't leave me.'

'Ambulance is on its way,' Moira said as she came close. She placed her hand upon Stella's shoulder. 'Is he...?'

'I don't know!'

Moira knelt by his side and placed her fingers on his throat. She had seen this in a movie. She exhaled loudly. 'I think I feel a pulse.'

Stella sat up and looked at her. She was as pale as freshly washed white linen. A faint light returned to her eyes. 'Really? You sure?'

'I'm no nurse. You check, too. Can't you hear his heart?'

'I'm shaking too much!' She stood up and screamed. 'Where is the ambulance?'

'Let me go inside and get some clothes for you.'

The ambulance sirens reached their ears as Stella put on her shoes. The ambulance's tyres screeched as it came to a halt. Two tall men jumped out of the back and rushed towards them.

Both rushed to Evagoras's side while asking questions about the incident.

'Just tell me he is alive. I don't know what happened.' The moonlight shone in Stella's tears. She spoke differently. Her facial muscles moved at a minimum. Her lips hardly ventured, and her eyes were still. She could not face her husband as he was lifted into the open ambulance. Moira knew the feeling well. She could not help but place her hand on Stella's shoulder. 'He is going to be fine.' A lie. She saw the pool of blood on the flat grass. She saw the head injuries. Even if he lived, he would not be fine. But Stella needed to hear such a line.

'You coming, ma'am?'

Stella remained motionless. Moira reacted instinctively and took her by her hand and led her to the ambulance. 'Can I come as well? She needs someone by her side.'

'Don't we all? Hurry up. Both in, now!'

Stella sat trembling with her eyes fixed on the man trying to save Evagoras. Needles, bandages, and tubes came and went. It all felt so surreal. As if watching a medical drama on TV. Her brain fought to distance itself from the pain and shock. 'Wake up, Evagoras! I can't raise two kids alone! I need you!' She was not sure if she whispered the words or if they were spoken inside her mind. Her pupils journeyed to the side, and she looked at Moira sitting by her side, holding her hand. '*Shut up, Stella, you fool. She is raising two kids alone!*'

Nine minutes and thirty-nine seconds later, Evagoras was rushed through the doors of Corfu's general hospital. Stella squinted at the bright white light as she trudged behind, like a zombie in those ridiculous movies Evagoras loved so much.

'Stay here!'

Stella obeyed. She remained standing still until Moira led her to a chair. They sat in silence. Stella with her gaze fixated on the fake bush in the brown ceramic pot opposite them, and Moira watching the TV screen hanging in the corner of the vast waiting room. Late night news. Tragic incidents played in tragic surroundings.

Stella finally moved when she felt the need to rub her aching back. The bumpy ride over and the hard, cold hospital chairs did not help with her chronic pains. Her eyes noticed the round clock on the wall above the nurses' front desk. The hands seemed to move slower. An eternity had passed inside her soul, yet it had been only twenty-five minutes since their arrival.

Suddenly, the doors to her right, screeched open and a tall doctor with small specs came walking out. She hated the smile on his face. It was fake. It carried sorrow. Stella began to shake her head. 'Please, no. Lord, no, please.'

The doctor knelt before her. 'I'm sorry, Mrs. We did all we could, but his injuries…'

The doctor continued talking, yet only white noise reached Stella's ears. Her man, her rock, her high-school sweet-heart was gone. She would never again feel his warmth up against her, smell his unique odour when his sweat mingled with his sweet cologne, laugh at his daft jokes, argue with him for meaningless reasons, watch him be a great father, nudge him to take out the trash, watch movies with ludicrous plots, cook pastitsio together… An entire life turned into a memory. No more future plans, except his funeral. Stella let out an animal-like cry and fell to the ground.

Stella woke up in a hospital bed with a heavy head, hours later. She knew time had passed as the sunrays invaded the room easily through the thin white curtain that was dancing upon the morning sea breeze.

Moira was awake on an old, worn-in burgundy armchair in the corner reading a mystery novel that she had picked up from the visitor's lounge.

'Good morning.'

'What's so good about it? Why am I here?'

Moira folded the edge of the page and closed her book. 'You fainted and then woke up screaming. You were given a sedative. Nurses brought you up. You don't remember?'

Stella shook her head. 'You've been here all night?'

'Armchair is far more comfortable than what it seems. Anyway, I had no way back and I thought you would want company on our way back to the mansion.'

'Thalia must be wondering where we all are.'

'If she remembers us.'

Stella fixed her posture and pushed back against her pillows. She did not feel like smiling but could not resist at hearing Moira's last sentence. 'Listen, Moira, I have nothing against you and thank you for your support. We are two widows with two kids each. I suggest we go back to Thalia and tell her that whatever her will is and whoever is on it, needs to change. She should sign it all over to our four children. Our four fatherless kids.'

Moira nodded in agreement. 'Let's call a nurse and see about getting you out of here.'

Greece and its paperwork.

It took the two women over two hours to find a nurse to check and note down her stats, to find a doctor to check the nurse's findings, to see the patient, to sign her release papers, to take the papers down to the reception and file them, and then complete all the necessary forms for Evagoras's body to be transferred to the morgue in Athens.

Just before noon, the two women exited the main entrance and beelined to the first taxi in sight. A plump man with a goatee and a checkered shirt that was untucked in multiple places and unable to enslave all the chest hair on a rampage. 'Good morning, ladies,' he said cheerily.

Moira just replied with the address and opened the door for Stella. She then turned towards the driver and added, 'A drive in silence, please. She just lost her husband.' Neither were up to listening to yet another know-it-all Greek taxi driver with a PDH in everything.

Moira paid the driver as the vehicle came to a halt outside the house. The main gate was open, and the front door unlocked from the previous night. Stella took one look at the dried blood sparkling in the sun and began to weep.

'Let's get inside,' Moira said and led her in by the shoulders.

'Thalia? Auntie Thalia?' Moira called out while Stella fell back onto the sofa and continued her cry.

Moira looked down the corridor. 'Auntie?' She rushed upstairs calling her aunt's name. Silence. 'Could she be out? I doubt she could still be asleep. She is probably in her garden. I hope she has not wandered off again,' she spoke to Stella as she reached the top. Stella did not reply. Moira knocked on her bedroom door. No reply. A minute later, she was running back down the stairs.

'She's dead!'

Stella wiped her eyes and sat up. 'What?'

'She's dead,' Moira repeated, pointing upstairs. 'In her bed. She looks asleep but I shook her, and she is cold as ice!'

Another ambulance set off for Thalia's mansion. The paramedics had changed shift. A short woman with brown, piercing eyes and platinum blonde hair rushed through the front door followed by her olive-skinned colleague with the thick moustache.

'Upstairs,' Moira said and her voice broke as she added, 'third door to your left', to the two professionals running up the stairs with their equipment in hand. Moira watched them go up while Stella remained still in the corner of the white sofa. She bit her lip hard hoping to wake up from the nightmare. But it was no dream. Thalia was confirmed dead. The coroner's report that came days later, brought some peace of mind as the medical examiner concluded that she died placidly in her sleep. Her illness had weakened her, eaten her up from the inside. The lawyer's conclusion though did not bring such peace to Stella.

They had called him right after the ambulance drove off carrying Thalia's lifeless body. A peculiar type of man with beady eyes, a long thick beard hung alone on an otherwise clean-shaved face and pointy gelled hair, much more fitting to a teenage boy had walked into the living room an hour later. He had worn a dark grey suit that did not flatter his pale-for-a-Greek complexion. A man in his early fifties; his cheap cologne had invaded the room, engulfing the fresh air.

'Morning, ladies. So, Mrs. Thalia's dead, huh?' He had not waited for a reply. 'Follow me. I need witnesses.'

In the master bedroom of the house, the two women had stood by the door and witnessed the strange man, after placing his hands on a replica painting of the last supper by

DaVinci, pick up the painting and reveal a small secret cupboard behind it. It was unlocked. Only a single piece of paper lay inside.

'Hmm. Seems like Moira gets it all. Which one of you two is that?'

Chapter Thirteen

Twelve hours back

Moira stood before the mirror in her en-suite. She exhaled and the glass fogged up slightly. 'You can do this.' She raised her hands, cracked her knuckles, and wore her black gloves. She opened her bedroom door with care. Her eyes travelled the length of the hallway, left and right. Everyone had just returned to their rooms. She tiptoed outside and headed to the last door on the right. A small cleaning closet. She quietly placed the bucket and mop to the side and approached the wall shelves. She pushed the toilet paper rolls aside and reached for the handle. Inch by inch, she pulled the secret door towards her. A dark corridor lay behind it. Faint light illuminated the floor.

Thalia always locked her bedroom door. Ever since her violent drunk father came in and pulled her out of bed by her hair, she had locked it. Moira watched her do so from behind a thin opening cleverly placed below a wall painting. She then saw Thalia remove the last supper and pull out many papers out of her safe. 'Goodbye, Paris,' she said and threw a piece of paper into the flames of her well-lit fireplace. 'Good riddance, Sebastian.' And another one turned to ashes. 'And finally, awful Moira. Fuck you!'

'Don't you move!'

Thalia jumped forward and let out a loud gasp. Moira stood behind her, pistol in hand. 'How did you...' Thalia looked at the secret door opened behind the lady. 'Oh, I see you found my secret passageway. Didn't think of you as smart.'

'I was suspicious when I saw the lines by the bookcase in the living room, but you knowing me cursing God got me thinking. At first, I thought secret cameras, but then I realized how smaller certain rooms are compared to the overall building. You brought us here to spy on us.'

'I don't know you lot well. I wished to see who would get my fortune. What kind of person will inherit my company stocks? I leave nothing to chance.'

'And were planning on leaving a sick widow with two kids with nothing. Ready to toss the will with my name on it to the flames.'

'You are an awful human being. Your suffering is well deserved.'

Moira took a step forward and shook her gun-holding arm. 'Very brave for a woman at the receiving end of a gun.'

'Oh, dear. I'm dying. I'm not a cat. No lives left. Are you going to kill me twice, thief?'

'Thief?'

'I see everything. Missing books, missing ornaments, my bracelet. All in your suitcase! You even took the silver spoon you ate with. Scum is what you are, Moira and you deserve to continue living as such. You and the kids you pushed out.'

Moira ran forward and pulled Thalia's head back by the hair while placing the cold end of the gun to her throat. 'Say no more, witch.' Moira took the will with her name on it from Thalia's hand and placed it back in the secret cabinet. She, then took out the only one left inside. Evagoras's.

And into the fire it went.

'Now, get into bed,' she ordered.

With Thalia tucked in nicely, Moira wished her a good night and placed a pillow over her face.

Moira watched as the old lady's body twitched and wiggled under the sheets. She expected to be more shocked. Close her eyes even. But no, Moira witnessed Thalia's entire ordeal. Not for a second did she blink or think of removing the pillow.

Time moved slowly as it does at such times. As if the brain protects itself by taking it all in gradually. Soon, Thalia was still. Moira raised the cushion and was surprised to see such a peaceful face staring back at her.

'No remorse. Life gave me shit. Time to start taking.'

Back through the secret corridors she went, ready for her next victim.

She waited patiently. Like a lioness stalking her prey from the shadows. With Stella in the bathroom and Evagoras standing by the open window, Moira decided to leap and attack. No need for the gun. No need for evidence.

And out Evagoras went.

Lady luck finally decided to give Moira a break.

The police never mentioned suspecting her as Stella clarified that their door was locked and that she saw Moira come out of her room to help, but Moira knew that with two dead bodies, the two living people in a house would definitely pass the investigator's mind as possible murderers.

However, the coroner's report on Thalia came back and stated that the sick old lady's system was ready to give up at any given moment. She had died peacefully in her sleep, he had concluded.

Moira's luck did not stop there. Evagoras had taken out a life insurance the previous year after he got a small raise at work. The sum was enough to pay off their apartment and set up -as he wished- two college funds for their children. After it was announced that Thalia had chosen Moira as her sole heir, Stella came to the conclusion that Evagoras must have found out that he was getting nothing and took the plunge. She knew that he was not going back to living poor. She knew that he wanted a better life for his kids. It all made sense to her and that is what she told the police, and the case was closed.

Still, Stella felt that she deserved something from Thalia's estate.

One sunny morning as she sat alone in her kitchen, frappe in her right hand, she picked up her phone and began to compose a rather lengthy text.

'Dear Moira, how are you? I am only now starting to find my footing again. It is a weird pain of hollowness that unfortunately you know well. Did you decide on the house? Did you move in or sell the place? Must be absolutely lovely to have the burden of providing for your two children lifted from you. Thankfully, due to the life insurance, I haven't got the loan pushing me down anymore, but as you know, it costs an arm and a leg to raise children properly... alone. At one point, we were going to share the estate and yes, Thalia chose you, but she did that before Evagoras died. She chose you because she knew you were a widow with two underage kids. That is what I am now. It is a shame that I was left out. That my children were left out. Of course, I don't ask for half. In fact, I will not even ask for much. Just enough to help raise my kids. Please, Moira, find it in your heart and see what you can do to help me. With all my love and gratitude, Stella.'

Stella must have re-read the text over five times, fixing it again and again. She wanted to get the wording exactly perfect.

She took in a deep and finally press the button to send it.

Minutes later, she noticed that Moira had received and opened her text. She tapped her fingers on the table and rocked back-and-forth as she eagerly waited for a reply. A reply that did not come that day. At night, after tucking her kids to sleep, Stella returned to her bedroom and fell face down onto her empty double bed. She hugged her husband's pillow and wept into it. It still carried his scent. She never washed his pillowcase. The scent had weakened but it was still there.

A reply came two days later.

'Okay. I'll see what I can do.'

Stella stared at the short text. She did not know how to feel. Happy that it wasn't a negative reply. Not a big fat no. Sad as the short message probably meant that Moira could not be bothered? Anxious that she did not mention how she was going to help?

Stella yelled and threw a vase against the kitchen wall. At least, the mess would give her something to do. After the clean-up, she texted back. 'Great. I knew I could count on you. You are an angel.'

And again, Stella waited. With every beep of her phone, her heart skipped a beat, yet Moira never texted back.

First of the month, there it was. A white envelope in the post. It was addressed to her. She ripped it open and took out the check.

'You got millions and you send me a check for five hundred euros? You cheap bitch...' Stella never swore. She placed one hand on her mouth and the other on her heart. *'Relax, Stella. This could be on a weekly basis. Could be some sort of dividend from stocks. Sums could get larger.'*

Weeks came and went, and no check arrived until the first of next month. Again, the same amount. Stella received five hundred euro a month for years. Up until her youngest turned eighteen. Then, in the envelope, she received a small note instead of a check. 'Your kids are now adults and have their dad's college funds. You need no more support.'

A new vase met the wall. Stella picked up her phone and called the mansion. The fact that a maid answered her call infuriated her more. 'Just give me Moira.'

She could faintly hear Moira whispering in the background to make an excuse. 'And always make an excuse when it's Stella.' She heard her last sentence well.

'Mrs. Mirela is busy at the moment...'

'Who?'

'Mrs. Moira does not use that name anymore. She finds her proper name more fitting to a lady of her status. May I take a message?'

'Yeah, tell the bitch that she has my curse and to go screw herself!'

Part III

RESOLUTION

Chapter Fourteen

Shocks (by general population standards) always failed to shock Damien. He did not know if it was his hard shell, thick skin, or numbed-by-the-alcohol brain. His go-to reply was a usual 'oh' and if you were lucky a slight nod of the head. That is what the foul news coming from Anneta received.

Damien was on his way back to the hospital to finally receive closure on the country mansion massacre when his phone began to vibrate on his dashboard. He pressed the button and silenced the car radio. He was not listening anyway. His mind was talking too much. It had been hours since his last drink and the drive to the hospital dug up memories deeper than an undertaker. Happy rides during the pregnancy, sorrowful ones during the cancer.

Anneta's voice dominated his inner thoughts.

'Damien? It's Anneta...'

He rolled his eyes. He hated how she announced who she was. Her name flashed on his phone. He had her cell number and desk number in memory. *'It's 2022 for crying out loud.'*

'…we couldn't locate the kid. Her other son. The number we were given goes straight to voice mail. OTE informed us that it has not been used for the last two months. I called his university and get this; he has not shown up for lessons for the last two months. I sent a local police car to his registered apartment. No one has seen him for…'

'The last two months.'

'Exactly. Damien, he must be our headless body in the basement. Age of the body fits. We should have thought of this sooner.'

'We went by the info of the nurse and the neighbors that he was away at uni. Sounds solid, but let's get a DNA comparison done with his sister and be sure about…'

'I am sure. The girl next door of his apartment mentioned that the last time she saw him was when they all went out and got tattoos done before heading to their towns for the long weekend. She said Theodore got a dragon done on his right arm. It's him.'

'Oh.'

The next shock of the day was not received so calmly.

Damien casually walked through the hospital doors and made his way to Zoe's room. He found it empty. The bed was bare. His heart sank. His fingers twitched. *'Fuck, no.'*

He grabbed a nurse walking by and startled her. 'Nurse, where is the lady that was in this room? Is she okay? They told me she just needed rest. Did she have another seizure? Talk, God damn it!'

The nurse pulled her arm back. 'Sir, calm down. I have no idea what you are on about. This isn't my floor. Go to the nurse's station.'

Her tone made him take a step back and take in a much-needed breath. He held out his right palm. 'I am so sorry,' he said and rushed over to the front desk to find out what had happened.

Mrs. Voula lowered her glasses. Damien had repeated his questions in the same fashion. 'Boy, relax. We just moved her to the fourth floor. She is no emergency anymore. Another couple of days and she will be free to go.'

'Room?'

'407.'

For the first time in years, Damien found himself running up the stairs. He had always been an elevator fan, but his love was not. They took the stairs together. She had put fitness in his life. He opted for the elevator every time since her death.

As he was about to rush into the room, he paused. He took in stale hospital air and let it linger in his lungs. He wiped his forehead and fixed his hair with his sweaty fingers. He took the next few steps up to room 407's door as if strolling through the park by his apartment block. He bent his fingers and knocked on the door. He heard a faint reply and entered. Zoe sat up on her bed, supported by three pillows. The thin kind that you encounter at cheap hotels and cheaper bazaars. The room was smaller but welcomed more daylight into it as it boasted two windows, one facing the east, the other smaller one to the south.

'Good morning.'

Zoe closed the magazine she was reading and placed it by her side. 'I heard I gave you a fright. A seizure as you were talking to me, I was told.'

'I don't scare easily. I was worried about your health.'

'Of course. You did not get the end of the story.'

Damien walked over to the bed and made himself

comfortable in the white plastic chair by her side. 'Do I seem so... how can I put it? Lacking human emotions? I was indeed worried...'

'I did not mean it to sound so judgemental. I just understand how important this is to you. You seem like the workaholic kind of guy.'

'I don't give out family man vibes? A happily married guy with three charming children whose work is just a means to provide to them?'

'Well, are you?'

'Nope. Married to murder cases and provider to only my dog.'

Zoe smiled and fixed her position amongst the pillows. 'I love dogs. My mother never let me have one. What dog do you have?'

'A German Shepherd.'

'Beautiful breed. Bit too hairy for a Greek island, though.'

'My thoughts exactly. So, what dog would you chose to have?'

'A Labrador surely.'

'Good choice.' Damien tapped his fingers on the bed's railing. 'Well, small talk is great and all...'

'But let's get to the final night, right?'

Chapter Fifteen

Zoe's eyes opened before her alarm clock went off. The joyful sensation that this fact used to bring her during her studying days was missing. She used to look at the time and with a smile on her face, she would change position and go back to sleep knowing she had another half an hour of slumber. Now, she sat up and sorrow was her dominant emotion. Her heart ached from beating so fast due to the lights and noises in the house from the night before. Her mind kept her up until her exhausted body forced it to shut down. She knew if she stayed in bed, she would only drive herself crazy with thoughts. 'Busy hands, quiet mind,' she repeated the wise line from one of the nuns. Sister Mary was the most serene old lady that helped out at the orphanage. Many troubled teens came and went, and sister Mary was the only one that managed to keep their rage locked away. She soothed them by keeping them busy. So busy that they had no time to think about the shitty hands that unfair Miss Life had dealt them. So busy that by night-time, and after a warm supper, they slept like baby swallows curled up below their mother's wing.

Zoe opened wide the windows and pushed the curtains back, allowing the sun's generous light to spread out in the room. Fresh air ventured in and filled her lungs. Zoe went about with her morning routine, singing softly to herself. She exited into the hallway, dressed in a colourful dress, wearing her favorite sneakers and a lipstick smile. She was not going to let anything keep her down. She had an interesting afternoon and night planned ahead. She prepared Mirela's breakfast tray and walked up to her door. She knocked once and entered without waiting for a reply.

'You're early,' Mirela grunted and then pushed herself up to an upright position. 'Why are you so cheery? Stop it. It's annoying at such an hour. I can still hear your awful singing vibrating in my ear. Made my veins pop.'

Zoe had no idea what she meant by that and thought that everything was annoying to Mirela at any hour of the day. Her thoughts though remained exactly that as she uttered an uplifting good morning while opening the window shutter. She then placed the tray on the special table and brought it in front of Mirela. 'Eat up now. Enjoy your coffee. Your pills are ready in the white cup. Here's your remote control. If you need anything just call.' She spoke fast and moved even faster. She was out of the room in a matter of seconds. A slight migraine was brewing due to lack of sleep and coffee, and she had no intention of letting her miserable boss bring her down.

Zoe sat down at the kitchen table with a hot coffee, a piece of toast and her cell phone. Mirela's son had not replied, while her daughter had finally texted that she would call later on as she was busy at work. The most important message though came as she was cleaning up.

'On my way, my love. Be there by late evening.' She read Leo's message three times and it excited her each time the same.

She did not hear from Mirela that morning at all. She enjoyed her book, an easy crossword, a long shower as to shave for the night, and prepared lunch. She put extra care into her meal making but was even more careful to place a Temazepam below her usual bunch of midday pills. Mirela enjoyed a nap after lunch on most days. Zoe did not wish to take any chances. It *had* to be a nap day. It had to be a longer than usual siesta. Zoe needed an hour or two. She was determined to find out more about Mirela after the incident with the ring and the lady at the gate, and she knew exactly where to go.

Zoe fed her patient while they both watched the notorious Greek gossip shows that haunted the airwaves between one o'clock and four. Such 'garbage' was not allowed at the orphanage, but Zoe loved to hear all about the rich and famous. What they wore, ate and talked about. Where they went and with who. The money, the sex, the cars, the houses, the fashion spiked her excitement.

'Your pills now, Mrs.' She passed Mirela the cup and quickly began to comment on the story with the drunk singer that crashed his new Ferrari into a lamppost.

'And your water.'

Zoe spoke about the TV, but her eyes watched as Mirela swallowed down the five pills. She stayed by her side, with an eye on the showbiz news and one on Mirela's drowsy eyes. She was asleep before the commercials.

Zoe switched off the television, took the tray back into the kitchen and headed out the door.

Greek mentality was the same over every inch of the small sun-kissed country with the hundreds of famous islands. If you wished to found something out, head over to the village square, find the oldest coffee shop -if more than one- and get chatty with the quiet old man in the corner enjoying his third hot Greek coffee or even better, the wife of the owner. Zoe was lucky that day. She walked through the narrow snake-like paved streets amongst the renovated country homes built after WWI and arrived at the picturesque town center at its most quiet time. Siesta. Pensioners were animals of routine. They visited the coffee shops early morning, then went about with their chores, went back for a second coffee and head home for lunch and a nap. It was during this nap time that Zoe strolled past the wooden woven chairs under the overgrowing pink bougainvillea and entered the sweet-smelling coffee shop of Saint Helen. A rich coffee aroma blended with the scent emanating from the flowers growing out of pots of various sizes and colors spread out throughout the shop and resting upon windowsills.

Zoe walked by the only two customers at the time. Two old, most likely near-centenarian men were preoccupied with an on-going game of Tavli -Greek backgammon as it is known in the English-speaking world. Zoe headed for the small round wooden table in the corner. A thin vase sat in the middle of the light green tablecloth and housed a single rose. Its yellow petals were as vibrant as the morning sun. Must have been freshly cut.

Zoe was sure that her presence would spike the interest of the owners. A man in his late fifties, offered her a wide islander smile that raised his thick greyish moustache. 'Good day, little Miss.'

'Good day, sir.' She spoke louder than usual as she could see the owner's wife cleaning some coffee cups in the back. Her volume worked just fine as the woman stopped what she was doing and looked over her shoulder. Soon, the stout middle-aged lady with the blue apron wobbled over to her table to take her order and extract as much information as she could. Little did she know that that was Zoe's initiative as well.

'So, what would a little sweet thing like you be having today?'

'Any chance of some orange juice? Oranges are entering their season.'

The short woman smiled. 'They sure are. I will freshly squeeze some right now. No city bottled stuff here.' She stressed the word city. She took a step back as to head back to the kitchen but as she did not receive a reply, she dared to ask. 'You're not from around here, are you? Don't mean to intrude but I know all the grandkids that still manage in their busy lives to visit their old folk.' She mocked the word busy.

Zoe smiled and looked straight at the woman. 'How about you bring over that juice and whatever you are drinking, and sit down with me for a chat? I haven't really got anyone to talk to if I am being honest.' Zoe saw the woman's face light up. She rushed back to her counter and returned shortly with the cold beverage, a plate of home-made cookies and her own green tea in a white porcelain cup with flowers painted by hand on the side.

'So, no one to chat to you say?' the woman with the dyed curly hair said as she placed the contents of the tray on the table and took a seat opposite Zoe. 'I'm Helen, by the way. So, what is a young girl like you you doing here in the outback all alone?'

Zoe took in a deep breath. 'I took a nursing position at the mansion on the hill. Mrs. Mirela if you know her.' Zoe let the words resonate. Mrs. Helen frowned and tried to control her facial muscles from clenching. She coughed before she spoke.

'And how are you finding it? Been here long?'

Zoe took a sip from her juice. It helped with her dry throat. It wasn't a long walk from the house to the village square, but the day was unusually hot, and Zoe was already sweating from the whole 'drug my boss-head to town-learn secrets' situation.

'Oh, no. Only been here a couple of days.' Another needed sip. 'But I do find your village a real beauty.'

'Hmm. And... err, how are you finding Mirela?'

Zoe thought carefully about her wording. 'Poor thing. Surrounded by riches and yet so sick and in need of constant care. Must be hard to be locked up there all day and not being able to come down here and socialize with the rest of you.'

'She was never one to socialize, child.'

Zoe dared to push the conversation further. 'Yes, she is quite a difficult character. And if I am being totally honest, from the look on your face, the postman's expression and my encounter with a neighbour, I am getting the sense that even if she were to socialize, she would not be very welcome. Not that I am saying you are not welcoming folk, of course.'

'Oh, child. You don't know the half of it. What neighbour?'

Zoe made the decision right there and then, to repeat the stolen ring incident. Mrs. Helen listened nodding her head so frequently that it reminded Zoe of the wobbly-headed dogs the bus driver to school had on his dusty dashboard.

'She even called her a murderer! Chilled me to my core.' Zoe fiddled with her chain and pulled out her cross from underneath her dress. She pinched her cross with her fingers. 'Lord, what have I gotten myself into?'

'Religious, huh? Glad to see in a girl your age. You don't get that often nowadays.'

Religious card dealt. Time for the sympathy card.

'Oh, yes. I was brought up by nuns, you see. I was an orphan. I knew from a young age that all I wanted to do was help others.'

'And you ended up with the awful sinner?'

Zoe wiped her eyes even though no tears had been produced. 'Oh, Mrs. Helen!' She lay her hand upon the woman's. 'Please, help me. Tell me. What have I gotten myself into to?'

Mrs. Helen looked around her even though she knew the two old men were deeply lost in their gamely battle and the peace and quiet coming from behind the counter meant her husband had retired for a short nap among their two poodles on their kitchen sofa.

'Well, I am not one to gossip but you deserve the truth. We need all parts of a story to be able to judge it. Hear me, child and make your choices. That house belonged for decades to one of the richest ladies on our island. Mrs. Thalia. A true beauty that one. She reminded me of Maria Callas when she stood proud and pierced you with those eyes of hers. A great woman that unfortunately never married.' Helen waved her hands. 'Yes, yes, I know that nowadays you young ones believe that happiness can be found elsewhere like in work and travelling, but I'm old fashioned. A woman is only complete when she has a household to maintain and raise children that she carried. Or not. Adoption is a Godly act and amazing to all parties involved.' She sighed loudly. 'There I go blabbering away. Stop me, child. Now, where was I? Oh, yes. Thalia. Thalia had no children and when she was hit by an awful disease many years ago, she invited her closest relatives to come stay with her. She wanted to see if any of them were worthy of her inheritance. Mirela, Moira back then, was Thalia's niece. She showed up here, dressed in black, pale as a ghost and gained our sympathy. You see, the people down here voted on who they thought Thalia would choose. A sick widow with a dead kid and not enough money to raise her two living ones, it seemed a sure thing that Moira would get a large slice of the pie. It the end, she took all the pie, but stories got around. Two days only Moira was in that house and her cousin who was the front-runner for the money, jumped out of the window ending his life. Thalia also died that night, apparently from fatigue due to her cancer and other issues. It could just be the bitter others, but gossip spread that Moira had something to do with both deaths. Stella, the leaper's wife, said that Thalia heavily disliked Moira and called her a thief.'

'A thief?'

Hellen nodded. 'Mmm. A thief. And that she truly is. She used to come down to the village in the beginning with her nose up in the air and wearing expensive clothes and jewellery, showing off to us peasants. Dislikeable to the bone. She only really spoke to a few ladies who were on the wealthy side of things. But that's when they started noticing precious things of theirs going missing. The village had a thief. When word got out and police started to journey up here, that is when Mirela stayed locked up in her mansion. She stated that her illnesses had got the best of her, and she was completely bed-ridden. A prisoner, she said. But a couple of weeks later, a ring and a bracelet went missing. And guess who was seen sneaking around the village late at night?'

'Mrs. Mirela?'

'Yes! Walking about just fine. A liar that one. A klepto-maniac liar. She loves to take and will never be satisfied with what she has gotten. No wonder, her children escaped as soon as they turned eighteen. Her daughter vanished down to Athens and we haven't seen sweet Alice since. Her son went off to study as far as he could even though we have a fine university right here in Corfu town '

'What a mess.' Zoe shook her head while Helen took a sip from her beverage. It had lost its steamy heat and was just the right temperature to allow the rich flavors sink in on the tastebuds.

'I saw stolen goods, you know. Jewellery with other names engraved on them.'

'Child, take them to the police.'

'I need this job.' The honest answer just came out of her.

'There are many jobs, young Zoe. Many houses with better owners for a girl like you. What if the rumours are true? What if she is a murderer?'

Zoe could not control a sharp shiver that ran down her spine.

'And don't forget,' Helen continued, 'she is most likely able to walk!'

Zoe returned home in similar fashion. In a rush. And now, with a heavier head. To her relief, the house welcomed her in complete silence. Zoe walked up to her patient's door and peeped through. Mrs. Mirela lay with her mouth wide open, drooling on her pillow. It wasn't until half an hour later that Zoe first heard her name being called.

'Bring me some water. My throat is completely dry. Why did you let me sleep in, girl?'

'You seemed like you needed it, Mrs.'

'That's for me to judge. Never let me sleep past four o'clock again unless told so. I will not go living like a bum. Then the illness wins.'

'Yes, Mrs.' Zoe began to ask her if she wished for an evening snack with her water, but Mirela just raised the remote control and turned on the fifty-inch television. The sound covered her voice. Zoe did not bother repeating her question. She went and came back with just the one glass, and quickly left the room. 'Leo is coming tonight. Focus there. Do not ruin your night of passion. Tomorrow morning, tell him everything and see what he has to say. Leo always knows best.'

Zoe fell back onto her bed and closed her eyes, daydreaming about how her prince charming would listen to her misfortune and sweep her off her feet, taking her back to his house to be his second wife.

Chapter Sixteen

Time seemed to move slower that evening. As if all the clocks in the house conspired against Zoe and purposely took their time conquering the minutes. Unfortunately for her, Mirela asked for a bath before bed. Zoe turned on the tap and watched as the hot water fell into the tub. The steamy cloud grew as she read Leo's latest message. 'On the boat! Final step! See you soon. XOXO'. She placed her hand upon her heart and closed her eyes. The ethereal mist swirled around her as she leaned over the tub and poured a special body salt into the water. It fizzled as it drowned, and a sweet aroma of berries emanated.

Zoe walked back into the bedroom and for a moment paused to look at her patient. She had to help her up and assist her to her bath, yet she could not shake the notion that Mirela could very well be able to walk. *'Maybe at that time when she stole, she could, but no more. She couldn't be such a good actress, could she? She must have gotten worse over the years. Small town gossip, that's what all this is!'*

Mirela smiled at the sight of her nurse standing in the

doorway. Zoe had never seen her smile before. She looked relaxed. A kind troubled lady in need.

'You sure look daft when you're thinking, child!'

And the wicked witch was back.

'Let's get you up, Mrs.'

'What are you thinking about? Men, I guess at your age. Feeling funny between the legs, huh? All alone up here, stuck with me and your stupid romance novels.'

Zoe took small steps as Mirela leaned on her. She did not know which sentence to comment on first. Her cheeks turned as red as the roses by the side of the mansion. Yes, she thought about men. Her man. Leo. *Vulgar woman talking about how I feel between my legs!* She thought about how easy it would be to just let go. Watch her fall to the ground. The hard, cold ground...

'Cat cut your tongue?'

'Its cat *got* your tongue.' Zoe sighed as she sat Mirela down next to the tub, to undress her. *But of course, you would change it to make it sound awful and macabre!*

'Mrs, how do you know the books I read are romance novels?'

Mirela's pupils trembled slightly. 'Err... what? I've seen you holding them around the house. That filth with naked cowboys on the front.'

Zoe was sure that she never held a book in front of her boss exactly because she knew the comments she would receive. She was careful on when and where she read. She examined Mirela's feet as she slowly took of her white, furry slippers. Swollen with thick, broken veins. Zoe was not convinced Mirela could walk. *Maybe cameras?* The thought scared her as her mind went to Leo and his night visit.

Zoe lowered Mirela into the tub and watched as her sore, aching, sickly-looking body sank beneath the bubbles.

'Some music, Mrs.?' Zoe was in no mood to engage in conversation of any sort with Mirela. She wished to maintain her high spirits. Mirela nodded. 'Anything from the golden years.'

Half an hour went pass before Mirela complained that the water was beginning to get cold. Zoe had almost fallen asleep on the green plastic chair by the tub. She had pressed play on a compilation of hits from the late sixties and early seventies, and after a few upbeat hits, it was mostly ballads about loves long lost and everyday hardships.

Zoe helped her up and with her holding on to the metallic railing with a tint of rust on its ends, she wiped her down and dressed her with her underwear and turquoise night gown. 'TV before bed, Mrs.?' Zoe asked as she tucked Mirela in. 'Of course. What am I? Eight? A kid on a school night? Why are you so eager to get rid of me? Got any plans?' Mirela's sinister laughter followed. Zoe held in her breath. 'No, ma'am. Just asking.' She switched on the television and placed the remote control by the pillow. 'I'll be back with your medication.' Zoe was back within a minute.

'Who are you? What are you doing in my room? Where is Michael?'

Zoe stood by the door with two cups, one in each hand. One with the pills, the other with the cool water. 'It's me, Mrs. Zoe. I was just here. Zoe? I have your pills.'

'Zoe? Your name is Alice, right?'

'That's your daughter, Mrs. I am your nurse.'

Zoe could hear the change in her own tone. She had no compassion left for Mirela. Guilt sunk in. She was a nurse. The woman's health and not character or past sins was what was important. She sat down by Mirela and stroked her hair back. 'Remember just now you were in the bath? What was that song that came on that you loved and started to sing? You have a beautiful voice, Mrs.'

'The Brightest Star by Aliki Vougiouklaki. You know, I named my daughter after the actress. So beautiful, so full of life. Everything I could never be. Now give me my pills and be gone. Show is back on.'

With the three night pills journeying down Mirela's throat and the screen showing late night variety shows, Zoe wished her a good night and retreated to her room. She was eager to call Leo.

One beep. And another.

'Come on...'

'Hello?'

Just his voice brought a smile to her face.

'My love. Where are you?' She whispered the words even though her bedroom door was closed, and she sat in her closet for extra noise cancelling.

'Speak up, babe. I can hardly hear you.' He shouted as winds could be heard swirling around him, screeching into the phone.

'Where are you?' she raised her voice.

'Arriving at the port. I can see Corfu as we speak.'

'Remember to get out further down from the gate. Don't come near the house. Text me and I will come meet you.'

'Yes, yes, my love. You worry too much. I remember from the first five times you messaged me so!'

His laughter was infectious. Her entire body felt its warmth. Uplifting. Joyful. Playful. She could describe his chuckles and giggles all day.

Leonidas 'Leo' Alexopoulos carefully placed his phone into his beige jacket's pocket and leaned on the railings. A row of lights stood in between the darkness of the sea and the night sky. Like beautiful stars gathered in a galaxy, the beach front properties of Corfu were well lit. Mostly restaurants, bars, shops, and cafes, they were in full swing at such an hour.

'Couldn't she have found a job in town? It's gorgeous here,' Leo spoke to himself as the ferry boat entered the port floating by an enormous cruise ship with an Italian flag on its side. 'No. It had to be a village in the middle of nowhere! Oh, Leo, man. You're nearly fifty! When are you going to stop chasing young girls all over the place?' He placed a cigarette between his lips and reached for his lighter. The wind was not planning on letting him indulge in his weakness. He headed behind a small lifeboat and squatted to avoid the breeze. His backpack got caught on a hook and as he tried to stand up, it ripped slightly on the side. 'Oh, come on. Oh, Zoe, our night better be worth it!' The ferry had stopped moving and the announcement from the speakers came shortly after. Soon, Leo found himself strolling the long promenade amongst locals and tourists, gazing around, taking in the magical ambiance of Corfu. A long line of taxis filled the road, each with its driver standing by its side waiting to pick up new arrivals and take them to town. Only Leo was heading away from the centre. Even the driver looked amazed. 'You from here? Visiting your grandmother?'

'Err, yes. Something like that.'

The next twenty minutes went by with the tall driver with the small goatee not pausing for air. He lowered the radio and went on to analyse everything from the economical crisis to the wars in Syria and Ukraine to the new facelift of singer Angela Demetriou.

Leo was not one for talking. He never cared for many male friends. He had a brother at a close age and a best man who he grew up with. He needed no more. He was always more interested in meeting and discovering members of the opposite sex. His life goal was to meet and be with as many as possible. He was on a good track, thanks to his deep dimples, athletic build and kind, mesmerizing eyes. A track ruined by the pregnancy of his then college girlfriend. They were married within the year and Leo found himself a greater love in life. That for his twin babies. A boy and a girl. He ruled out divorce the moment he laid eyes upon them. He wanted to be a father to them. Hands-on, 24/7. So, he stayed with Maria and portrayed the happily married man well. However, inner instincts are hard to contain. He seized every opportunity he could for sex. Gullible girls that craved attention. Zoe was not his first affair. Little did he know though, as he stepped out of that taxi on that warm spring night that she was going to be his last.

Zoe could not keep still. After she had finished with her makeup and applied her new lipstick, she paced up and down in the room, phone in hand. She had checked it numerous times in the last five minutes and loathed it for its silence. As her palms began to sweat, her cell vibrated. A text. 'I'm here. By the lamp post, behind the bushes.'

Her fingers trembled as she texted. 'Don't move. I'll be there in five.' She corrected her grammatical mistakes twice before pressing send.

Zoe crept down the hallway and just like previous nights, she opened Mirela's door slowly. The lights from the television danced upon her sleeping face. As Zoe switched off the TV, she could hear Mirela's mellow snoring. With a smile upon her face, she fixed her patient's blanket and tiptoed out of the room, closing the bedroom door behind her.

The front door was heavy and quite loud. Zoe opted for

the side door of the kitchen. Aluminium did not creak. With her heart pounding beneath her chest, she dashed out into the night. The night flowers by the walls had opened and were worshipping the nearly full moon. She stopped at the gate. Her hands ran though her hair, quickly fixing it. She took in a deep breath and opened the gate. Leo's figure could be seen, standing in the light, enjoying a smoke.

'Leo?'

He turned around, threw his cigarette to the ground, and ran toward her. He picked her up, his hands nesting below her bottom. His lips attacked hers and Zoe felt lost and free.

'Mmmm, you taste like cherries.'

'New lipstick,' she giggled.

'God, I've missed you,' he said and placed his large hands in her hair.

'Missed me? You think as much as I have craved you? I've been so lonely up here.'

'Take me to your room, Miss, and I'll show you how much I have truly missed you.'

Zoe could feel her insides melting But her mind pulled her back to reality.

She took his hand and looked into his eyes. 'Listen, the old lady is asleep, but she is a nasty, wicked woman and trust me, she will go mental if she sees me bringing a man into the house. You must be absolutely quiet as we go in. Not a single word until we reach my bedroom and even, then as quiet as possible.'

'Is she really such a bitch?'

'Oh, Leo. You don't know half of it.' Zoe felt like falling into his arms and weeping, but she knew well enough to not ruin the sexual mood with her worries Leo was there to stay for two nights. She had time to talk things over. Time to explain her situation. Time to ask him to leave his wife now his kids were finishing with their studies and hopefully moving out. 'She is notorious in the village as a murderer and a thief.' She tucked on his hand and led him up to the gate. He could not stop chuckling. 'Oooh, a killer granny! Poor me! Where are you taking me, demon? Into the haunted mansion?'

'Be serious. We run to the side and enter silently! Stop laughing!'

The house welcomed the two lovers as they made their way through the dark corridor and into Zoe's bedroom. Leo immediately began caressing her body and kissing her neck.

'Wait.' One word. Breathless. She rushed to light the two scented candles she had bought for the occasion from the local store down in the village. Vanilla and cinnamon were not her top choices, but the only ones available. By the time she had switched off the lights and locked the door, Leo had undressed and lay completely naked on top of her bed. The image of his bare body gave her shivers. She undressed to her black underwear and walked toward him. She stroked his leg and she climbed on to the bed and smiled at the sight of his shaking erection. She ran her hand all along his leg until she reached her target.

'Oooff. Your hands are cold.'

'Then warm me up,' she whispered in his ear as she filled up his embrace.

Leo rolled her over and worked her body with his lips and hands. Soon, she was naked, and Leo entered her slowly. Zoe bit her lower lip and imprisoned her passionate breathing. Her fingers grabbed onto the magnolia sheet, and she closed her eyes as Leo picked up the pace. She turned her head sideways and sank into her pillow. As she opened her eyes, she saw it. It made her freeze on the spot.

The shadow below her door cutting the thin line of light into two.

'What's wrong?'

She placed her finger on his lips. 'Ssshh. Someone's outside our door.'

Leo lowered down and brough his lips to her ear. She could feel his hot breath as he spoke. 'I thought you said she couldn't walk.'

'Rumours say she can.'

They remained silent with their eyes fixated on the door.

Leo pulled out of her and sat by her side. A minute -one of those minutes that seem everlasting- passed before the shadow moved away. Faint footsteps were heard and then a closing of a door.

'Let's give her time to go back to sleep, huh?' Leo said, having caught his breath, 'Can I smoke at the window?'

Zoe nodded and stood up, looking for her underwear. She wore her robe on top and smiled at the sight of Leo's bare bottom by the window. He blew out a large cloud of smoke through the open window as she unlocked the door and looked outside. The corridor was silent. Empty. Zoe wondered if she should switch off the lights. Mirela insisted most lights stayed on overnight. At first, Zoe thought it was a security thing. Now, she had her doubts. *'Lights off, no shadow to be seen. Let her be outside my door. It's locked. What would she do?'*

Zoe walked up to Mirela's closed door and knelt. Curiosity had gotten the best of her once again. The night lamp on the bedside table offered abundance light for her to see through the keyhole. Mirela slept. She seemed in deep sleep. So peaceful that it worried Zoe. *'Could there be someone else wandering the corridors?'*

With her hand upon her heart, she switched off the

lights and rushed back through the dark to her room. With the door locked behind her, Zoe exhaled all the gathered air and tension.

'She's asleep. Or she is winning the Oscar this year.'

'So back to business or do you want to give her more time?'

Zoe walked up to him and placed her head upon his hairy chest. 'Screw her. I have had enough. End of the month when I get paid, I am out of here.'

Leo placed his hands on her head and kissed her forehead.

'Come back to Ioannina.'

'And be with you?'

He took a moment, but finally answered. Zoe finally heard the words she longed to hear. Lie or not, it woke the butterflies inside her stomach.

'And yes, be with me. Always. I am yours.'

He pushed the window closed, picked her up and rushed to the bed. The two lovers fell onto the bed and picked up where they left off.

Slight creaking from the bed and controlled gasps of joy covered the sound of footsteps from inside the room. The shriek that followed though, could not be covered.

'Rape! Rape! Get off her you filthy beast.'

Both jumped in pure horror. Their eyes opened wide as they saw the figure of Mirela in the dim candlelight. Zoe curled up by the bed's headboard and pulled the sheet around her.

'Now listen here, Mrs. You have no right...' Leo began to say as he walked on his knees upon the bed and raised his arm, pointing his finger at her.

'Rapist!' Mirela screamed and raised the sharp butcher's knife in her right hand. 'Stay away from me, you monster,' she yelled as she chopped off Leo's hand from just above the wrist. Blood shot out and sprang into the air coloring the bed sheets red. Warm blood splatted upon Zoe who screamed at the sight of Leo's hand falling to the bed.

Leo stared with an open mouth at his cut arm in disbelief. As if his mind did not allow for the pain to register just yet. He gasped for air. 'No, no, no. This can't... You bitch...'

Mirela laughed, picked up his hand and began to walk to the door.

Leo felt drowsy and weak but found the strength to follow her. 'Come back here!' he demanded. Mirela was unlocking the door when he shouted to her. She turned around and as if it was the most natural thing in the world, she lodged the knife into his chest, piercing his beating heart. Her facial expression did not change as she pulled out her weapon and swung it into his neck. Leo's lifeless body fell back and hit the bed; his hollow gaze right below Zoe. Zoe breathed hysterically and stood up. An animal like scream escaped her trembling lips as she chased Mirela.

'You killed him! You psycho!' she yelled but Mirela kept on going down the hallway. 'I'm going back to bed. A simple thank you for getting that filthy dick away from you, will do.'

Zoe shook her head in disbelief. Tears ran freely and she felt her heart ready to burst out of her chest. 'I'm calling the police.'

Mirela stopped by her door. 'Go on then.' She threw Leo's hand at her. 'Call them. Let them come. And who do you think they are going to believe? I can't walk, remember? All I will say, is that I saw you sneak in a man, and you were carrying a knife. You always took it to your room for protection. I heard you fighting. I heard him scream when you stabbed him. Oh, yes. That is exactly what I will say. And no more. I will lose my memory right on cue if they want details.' Her laughter was the last straw.

Zoe clenched her fists and contemplated an assault. But her logic prevailed. 'Good luck with that story, old witch. I have it all on camera. We were recording ourselves on my phone. Enjoy the rest of your pitiful life in jail!'

Zoe turned to re-enter her room and lock herself in while she called the police when she heard the running footsteps. Mirela had a second knife. A smaller one but just as sharp. She charged at Zoe. Zoe managed to step aside and pushed Mirela into the cabinet. Mirela fell, hitting her head hard on the edge of the wooden furniture. Mirela crawled away on all fours while Zoe picked up the knife, following her. 'Who's laughing now, bitch? Where are you running to? Soon, you will be locked away for good.'

Mirela made her way all along the hall and rested upon the wall. She sat up and breathed with difficulty. She looked up with a bloody face at Zoe towering her with the knife. 'Kill me and you will never be the same. Trust me, I know.'

Zoe raised the knife and smiled. She leaned forward and whispered, 'I'm not like you. Death is an easy way out. I want to see you suffer. No one will serve you well in prison. Shit food and wetting yourself in a cockroach-infested cell is your future.'

'Stay away from my mother!'

The voice from behind her, startled her. She swung around to see a woman around her height approaching her fast.

'Mother? Alice?' Zoe took a step forward, forgetting she was holding a knife and standing in front of bleeding Mirela. Alice grabbed her hand and lowered it, pushing the knife into her leg. Zoe twitched and shivered from the excruciating pain of the whetted, honed blade as it pierced through her skin and touched her bone.

'Let me explain,' she said in a gasp as she fell to her knees. Alice pulled out the knife causing Zoe to cry out. As Alice raised the knife, Zoe had had enough. With Leo's image in her head, she found the strength to leap up and push Alice back by the hands. The two fought over the knife, falling back to the ground. The knife slid away from them both. Rolling around, grunting, the very few seconds seemed like hours. Alice was stronger and soon, her hands were around Zoe's neck, pushing down with force. Zoe remembered the time she fell into a pond during a field trip with the orphanage. She never did learn how to swim. Soon, she was under water. The lack of air was the worst pain she had ever experienced. Her prayers to never feel such an ordeal went unanswered as on that tragic night, she felt her body craving once again for oxygen. Her eyes began to close as life began to leave her when she felt the handle of the knife. Her fingers walked along the grip. With her eyes still closed, she took a swing with the sharp blade. Alice's hands let go off her throat and Zoe gasped for air. Panting she pushed herself back and opened her eyes. She covered her mouth in horror. The knife was lodged into Alice's chest. Alice trembled and choked as she took a couple of small steps back before collapsing to the ground. Zoe looked away, only to see Mirela sitting still. She had also stopped breathing.

Chapter Seventeen

'That is when I heard your car outside. I pulled myself up from the hell and escaped that mausoleum.' Zoe brought a tissue to her eyes and wiped her tears.

Damien placed his hands upon his head and exhaled with a loud noise. 'What a night!' He placed his hand upon Zoe's. Hers were warm compared to his always icy fingers. 'You were so brave to re-tell what you lived through.' He smiled. He was not sure if he was smiling at her for support or because he was glad to have finally gotten the full story and what was better, it checked out perfectly with the crime scene. The bodies and causes of death all backed Zoe's story.

One detail though was missing.

'So, you knew nothing about the body in the basement?'

'Body in the basement?' Zoe's jaw dropped. 'What?'

'We found a body in the basement. Been dead a few months. Young man in his early twenties. Turns out it was her son.'

Zoe covered her mouth and began to weep. Soon, she

was crying uncontrollably. 'Where in hell was I living? How did I get mixed up in such a place?'

Damien sat up the bed and took her into his embrace. 'There, there. You had no idea. It was just a job.'

'I'm never trusting people again.'

Damien felt that he had crossed the boundaries and a small jolt inside him made him quickly stand up. He scratched the back of his head and said, 'don't let the bad mess up your view of the world.' He controlled a bitter snicker. *'That's rich coming from you, Damien!'* He coughed to clear his throat and added, 'You're young. You have your entire life in front of you. Humans are best at moving on.'

'Do you really believe that?'

'No.'

Both laughed as car horns echoed from the street below.

'No, but even if you carry the darkness in you, you can still create light.' Damien's honesty continued. He felt as if he was talking to himself. 'Find someone that makes you want to move on. Or a place. Or a hobby. There has to be more to life than this.'

Zoe sat up straight and took a good look at the peculiar detective philosophising across from her hospital bed.

'You're probably right. I've never really taken time for myself. To find out who I really am.'

Damien sat down in the tall-back armchair. 'Never had something you were really good at that only offered you bliss?'

'Surfing and diving. They make me feel free and alive. Maybe I will take your advice on a new place. I hear Koror Island is fabulous this time of year.'

Damien tapped his fingers on the armchair. 'Koror Island?'

'Oh, it's a diving paradise in Palau.'

'Heard of it, no clue where that is?'

'Pacific. Micronesia?' She read his blank expression. 'Near Indonesia? The Philippines?'

Damien nodded. 'See? You're already happier. Just talking about it...'

'And what are you really good at?'

'Drinking. Got a PHD and everything.'

He forced himself to laugh along with her sweet giggle and stood up. 'From what I have been told, you have a couple more days in here to go. I will type your story up and bring it over for you to sign.'

'And then?'

'Then you will be released on probation...'

'Probation?'

'Well, its an open case. We will take it before a judge and he or she will rule you innocent on counts of self-defence.' He read her look. 'You have nothing to fear. You are a victim here. Don't you forget that.'

'Thank you.' She licked her dry lips. 'Thank you for everything. Your support is much appreciated.'

Damien patted her bed and stood up. 'See you later, Miss Zoe.'

As he opened the door, he heard her voice. 'I wish we met under different circumstances. Better circumstances.'

'And which would those better circumstances be?' he asked, with his back turned to her. His hand was on the door handle.

'Let me continue my dream. I read about this beach on Koror called Long beach. If you google it, it shows the most beautiful beach your eyes will ever see, and we are Greek. We know our beaches. There are some colorful wooden benches below palm trees where you can sit and gaze at the sun dancing upon the waves of the turquoise waters while sipping Pina Colada in the shade. That is where I would have liked to have met you. In your red swimming trunks, black shades upon your thick hair, holding them in place as the breeze worked the palm trees and barefoot in the golden sand. You would approach me with happier eyes and relaxed shoulders. Not this bundle of stress and sorrow.'

'Bundle of...?' Damien laughed out loud and looked behind him. 'You surely have a way with words. See you later, Zoe.'

'See you later, Lieutenant.'

Damien drove back to the station with Koror Island on his mind. Behind his computer, he searched Palau and scrolled though various pictures of the Pacific paradise before opening a new Word document. He had a large report to type. He spread out his notes, opened the autopsy files and photographs from the scene and began typing away. The medical examiner confirmed that the son in the basement was stabbed with one of the kitchen knives. 'Whoever wounded Theodore -most likely his mother- did the deed, then returned to the kitchen, washed the knife and placed it back into the set,' he mumbled as he typed.

A freak for detail, Damien took hours to type reports. He reread each paragraph before proceeding to the next. Then, he reread the entire document fixing spacing and syntax issues. His next move was to sit back in his worn-in office chair and close his eyes to replay the case in the movie theatre of his mind. If it all made sense, satisfied, he saved the document and pressed on print.

His eyes followed the thin bright line of light as it printed out the eight-page report. Printed on both sides. Things got strict during the crisis. Mistakes were frowned upon by the Chief. 'Economy on all fronts,' he had declared in a station meeting with the same passion of a general sending his troops to war. 'Do not waste my budget!' The ending of Arabica coffee and its replacement with a nameless cheaper one that came in a big brown bag was the biggest hit in the war to save every last cent.

Damien held the report and walked up to the Chief's office. He knocked and waited to hear his boss's voice. The Chief was on the phone. Damien smiled as he was set to avoid any sort of conversation. He dropped the document on the mahogany desk and took a few steps back. He was nearly at the door when he heard the Chief whisper. 'All good, Damien?' He held his hand above the phone while still having it in his ear.

'Excellent,' Damien mouthed.

'Take the rest of the day off. Tomorrow, too. Present from me.'

Damien could not argue with that. He mouthed a sincere thank you and even bowed slightly. In a matter of seconds, he had already planned out the rest of his day. After a quick cigarette in the parking lot, he drove to his favorite kebab shop. Two doner kebabs, one pork, one chicken, both with everything plus extra Tzatziki. His order. Then one with only meat in in. Nothing else. Jolie's order. Last minute, he added a large portion of fries.

Damien hated many things in life. Traffic jams when carrying hot food home was toward the top of the list. He despised cold food with a passion. As he arrived home and unlocked his door, he felt the food. Much to his delight, it was still warm. He heard Jolie growl as he closed the door behind him. She was not expecting him at such an hour. He could hear her steady footsteps approaching, ready to attack. He put her out of the tension and whistled cheerily. She came running while barking happily, her nose exploring charcoal-meaty aroma escaping the plastic bag in her owner's hand.

Damien placed the bag out of her reach and ordered her to sit. He took off his shirt and unbuckled his belt. Soon, he was in his blue boxers and black socks. 'Come on, girl.' Damien sat on his bed with his back against the board while Jolie settled by his side. He picked up the remote control and while waiting for the streaming service to open, he unfolded Jolie's lunch. With the war movie playing, he bit into his food. Eating in bed with a good film on was one of his guilty pleasures -and Damien had many of those. Jolie finished hers and began to lick the paper as to get every piece of deliciously cooked pork. She then, jumped off the bed. Damien could hear her slurping away at her water bowl. He opted to wash his kebabs down with the bottle of whiskey on his bedside table. The movie was worth its long running time. Any movie that grabs you, makes you care about the fate of its characters and even causes a grown man's eyes to water up, deserves all the awards thrown its way. Damien switched off the television and darkness returned to the room. He had not bothered to open the blinds. He pushed the take-away to the floor and rolled to his side. With his stomach filled with booze and fast food and his mind filled with images of World-War II, Damien slept for six hours straight. Two more that he slept on most nights.

Damien awoke after the sun had vanished behind Corfu's rugged hills and the moon was halfway to its throne in the night sky. As soon as Jolie sensed her master move, she picked up her leash and rushed to his side. She danced around, wagging her tail as he dressed.

May carried a chilly air to it. It was much welcomed though after the heat of the day and locals knew well that with June arriving, menacing heatwaves would be attacking soon. It was one of the last few nights when you could go for a walk without sweating. 'Come on, girl,' he urged her as she sniffed around among the tall grass to find a place to relieve herself. 'Daddy's going out tonight!'

Damien's attire was in full contrast to the old tracksuits and ripped sneakers he wore to walk Jolie. Navy blue trousers, brown belt and shoes, a white shirt and a generous splash of Eros by Versace, and Damien was out the door.

A bar on the outskirts of town, further down from the port, in an area mostly inhabited by warehouses, office buildings and large DIY stores, was Damien's top choice for a night out alone. He knew the owners, the bartenders, and the waiters well. They knew his big bills and generous tips. The entire place seemed to have time-leapt though a wormhole from the early 1980s and its many red lights -outside and inside- gave away its purpose. Men looking to get lucky, women looking for victims to squeeze cash out of. Both satisfied in the morning. A rather sad win-win situation.

The night did not go as Damien's many past nights there. His mind saw Zoe on every face he saw. She was the girl at the edge of the bar, the girl in the red dress clumsily carrying three beers, and the girl with the long legs burning up the dancefloor while drunk men threw carnation flowers at her.

'Another double, Bill.' But no number of doubles took Zoe off his mind. The usual numbness came, and Damien was shocked to find that a new woman occupied his thoughts.

He did not approach any woman that night. He even brushed off a couple who made attempts at starting a conversation with him. For once, he found himself relaxed. The bar was no longer a hunting ground for the opposite sex, a battlefield to conquer a sexual partner. For the first time, he enjoyed his drinks slowly while tapping along to the beat. He mouthed favorite lyrics and chatted away with Gianni, an old classmate of his and one of the three owners of the establishment.

He went home alone. None there were Zoe. None had her smile, her eyes or talked like her.

'Could she be the one to make me move on? Can I move on?'

Questions asked to a sleeping dog as he tiptoed by her to his bed at four o'clock in the morning. He picked up a packet of sour cream Pringles and a bottle of whiskey from the kitchen and headed to his bed. He switched on the television, mostly for light and background noise. Repeats of soaps were on. He did not expect anything else.

Half a bottle later, he devoured the last thin chip. Dizzy, he found himself watching the episode on the TV. 'Dumb show,' he whispered as he continued drinking. 'I'm drunk and even I can tell that she is sleeping with the gardener, you fool!' He loved speaking to the television. It was something his grandmother used to often do. 'Oh, come on. She's not your friend.' Damien rolled his eyes at the stupidity of the screenplay. Yet, sleep had not come for him. He felt wide awake. His hand entered his boxers as he contemplated masturbating to relax. He picked up the remote control and as he was ready to switch to porn, he heard the line.

The woman on tv said it. He quickly sat up straight. She said it again.

'I am from Nurses, SOS. Nurse Helena at your services, sir.'

He pressed the red button and silence and darkness returned to the room. His right hand searched amongst the sheets for his phone. He opened search and typed in Nurses, SOS.

'...a fictional agency in the universe of soaps created by director Lavrentis Papakaliatis. The agency of nurses features in both of his biggest hits, Shine and Good morning, Greece...'

Damien dropped the cell and brought his hands to the sides of his head. 'What the actual fuck?' He shook his head. 'Could it be the trauma? Did she confuse the agencies? Could not remember the real one and her brain filled in the blanks? Why lie?' He picked up his phone again. 'Maybe there is a real agency by the name. Some twat naming it after the show to gain customers...'

He searched but all results led to the fictional agency. He called up police HQ and got connected to the electronic police department. A sleepy voice answered his call. 'Don't laugh, but I need expect confirmation. Can you look through all business in Greece and see if there is an agency called Nurses, SOS?'

'Stay on line.'

The rest of the whiskey vanished as he waited. For results that did not make him feel any better.

'Why did Zoe lie?'

His last words as he finally fell asleep.

Chapter Eighteen

Damien awoke by Jolie's wet nose pushing against his bare foot. She was weeping for a walk. 'Just a sec, girl.' He jumped out of bed, stroked her hair, and quickly went about with his morning routine. In a matter of minutes, he was dressed and walking his dog out the door.

'Come on, girl,' he urged her as she fussed about her toilet spot. 'Daddy has places to be!'

Damien opted for a drive up to the mansion. He wanted to make sure before confronting Zoe. He was planning on asking her out and did not wish to blow his chances with worthless accusations. '*She was stabbed and witnessed a massacre,*' he excused her in his mind.

Damien drove up to the silent house on the hill and parked right outside the front door. He ducked under the police tape and opened the unlocked door. He headed straight to Zoe's room. He remembered a bunch of papers and cards in the top drawer of her bedside table. He sat on the edge of the naked bed. The bloody sheets had been collected as evidence. The red stains were there forever though.

Delivery menus, scribbled notes about pills, the daughter's phone number on a piece of paper and an agency card. 'Bingo!' His photographic memory served him well once more. 'Frontida.GR. Nurses for every purpose,' he read the card and began to punch in the number.

The cheery voice answered just after two rings. 'Frontida.GR. How may I be of assistance?'

'Err, yeah, hello. I am Lieutenant Damien Levante with Corfu Police. I know privacy and all, but I only need one small detail. Can you check a name and just tell me if she is a nurse of yours?'

A long pause followed. 'Maybe it would be better if you sent a formal letter or email so we can be sure you are with the police?'

'It is a murder case, Mrs. Time is of the essence here. I just need to know if she is one of yours.' He then said the sweetest please he could muster. 'And I will get the department to send in a formal request.'

'What's the name?'

'Thank you, thank you. Zoe Misiaouli.' He could hear the lady typing.

'Yes, she is registered with us. Is she okay?'

'A triple murder case in the house of the woman *you* sent her to take care off.' Damien knew exactly what he needed as a reply and emphasized the 'you'.

Another long pause. The woman replied with a crackling voice. 'Sir, we did not send her. These young nurses register with us but to be honest we prefer to send our more experienced nurses. We must be swamped to send one so young. Up to now, Zoe Misiaouli has not worked for us.'

She wanted to distant her agency from a brutal murder

case which on that morning would escape the small boundaries of the island and become headline news across Greece. Damien despised journalists more than the cockroaches that roamed his kitchen at nights. He was not looking forward to the media mayhem that was about to follow. At least, Anneta enjoyed the cameras. She could answer their questions as he stood silently in the background.

'Thank you, Mrs.'

Damien sat down in the armchair in the corner and gazed out the window. The colors of Greece filled his view. A country so bright and vibrant, you would think acts of darkness would not take place here, yet Damien had seen it all. Murders, rapes, mutilations, abuse, robberies, arsons, you name it. He had little faith in the *colors* of mankind. They did not deserve such a paradise. Maybe it was time God kicked them out like a bunch of ungrateful Adams and Eves. Maybe he needed to stop coming up with such weird thoughts. He tapped his fingers and brought his phone back to eyesight.

'Someone must know who sent her here.'

He looked across at the cross nailed to the wall. As he was about to sarcastically ask Jesus if he had any ideas, his eyes lit up. 'The nuns! Thank you, JC.'

His excitement did not last. After a few minutes of introductions, he heard the head-nun say, 'we haven't been in touch for the last couple of years.'

'*Shit!*'

'She called in the beginning of her studies but then these young birds need to spread their wings,' the slow-talking nun continued. 'Start living their lives without our support. From what I know though, both our girls got their degree.'

'Both?'

'Yes, yes. Zoe and Antigone. Best friend for years in here. Both went off to become nurses. They lived together and from what I know, they are still roommates.'

'Do you have a number for this Antigone?'

'Let me open my notebook, sir. I have their house number somewhere written down here. Those devil's smart phones are not for a lady of my age.'

Damien punched in the number, thanked the nun, asked for her blessing as his grandmother taught him to and quickly dialled Zoe's friend.

The rush of adrenaline and the anticipation pulled him out of the comfort of the chair and got him walking around. 'Come on, come on, pick up!'

He was about to give up as he passed the living room fireplace and was admiring Mirela in the photos. A strong, Greek look in her eyes. A proud mother of her boys. None of her daughter. *'She must have been in the empty frames. Sour history there for a mother to remove you from the family photos.'*

His thoughts were interrupted by Antigone who had picked up the phone. The ringing had woken her. She had been out clubbing the night before and was feeling the weight of her four glasses of wine. 'Who the heck uses land lines? And why hasn't it stopped ringing?' she said as she had forced herself out of her warm bed.

'Hello?' she asked in a slightly angry tone as she rubbed her right eye with her palm.

'Good morning, Miss. This is Lieutenant Damien...'

Antigone sat down. Her restless mind always rushed to the worse. Did one of her friends get in trouble last night? Crashed their car? Raped?

'...with Corfu Police...'

'Corfu? This is Ioannina. You must have the wrong

number,' she said with obvious relief. Antigone then gasped. 'Fuck! Zoe? Is this about Zoe?' She could not believe her mind only travelled to last night. Zoe. Her Zoe. She was in Corfu. Now, her brain went into overdrive. 'Is she okay? What happened? She is my roommate, but I am family. Her only family. You must tell me. Did that witch hurt her? Leo?'

'*You know all that and yet, she did not call you from the hospital,*' Damien thought as he stepped outside for a smoke. 'She is fine. There was some trouble here at the house she was working in. I am just calling to find out how she got the job as the agency has no clue.'

'Oh, after I got a job here at the local hospital, Zoe put an ad up on a couple of webpages offering her services. The lady's daughter called her. What was her name? Alice. Yeah, Alice, that's it. But why don't you just ask Zoe all about it?'

'Thank you for your assistance, Antigone.'

'Wait. Is Zoe okay? Tell me. Her phone has been off since yesterday. What aren't you telling me?'

'Have a good day, Miss.'

'No, wait!'

Damien ended the call and cursed loudly in the empty room. With his car keys rattling in his hands, he ran outside, slamming the door behind him. His brain went into over-drive as he sped down the motorway going nearly double the allowed limit. He took in a deep breath through the nose and held the air in. 'All your answers are waiting for you in that hospital room. What's the point in analysing why she lied? Zoe's secrets must have meaning to the story...' Damien touched his infotainment screen. 'Telephone. Call Anneta,' he ordered his vehicle's voice command. The radio was immediately silenced, and loud dialling tones replaced the coffee advert playing at the moment.

'Hello? Damien?' Anneta's voice came blaring through the car's eight speakers.

'Anneta, I'm driving right now so please, remind me. Did we find anything peculiar on Zoe's phone?'

'Peculiar, how?'

'Text messages with Alice, Mirela's daughter. Quite a few phone calls, for sure, right?

'Nothing of the sort. No communication was found between the two. Zoe only texted and called her roommate and her boyfriend while in Corfu. Especially with her roommate, she had frequent and lengthy calls.'

He ground his teeth. 'Okay, thanks.'

'I did find rather strange though that she had zero pictures in her gallery.'

'Zero?'

'Yep. Why are you asking?'

Damien swirled his car into an empty parking spot outside the hospital. 'I'll call you in a bit and let you in.'

Damien dashed into the reception area and went straight for the stairs. He pulled the heavy wooden door open and ran up. Sweating slightly and breathing rapidly he ran toward Zoe's room. Just as he was about to enter, he paused to collect himself. *'Don't come off aggressive. There could be a logical explanation to her nurse-agency lie. Stop getting worked up. Grabbing any excuse floating in the wind to see her again!'*

He knocked and as no reply came, he pushed open the door a few inches. 'Miss Zoe? It's Lieutenant Damien...' he began to say before realizing he was entering an empty room. The bed was bare, and the floor looked wet. The open window allowed the breeze to ran freely. It brought an odour of wild roses to his nose. *'A rather good detergent for a public hospital'*. Damien chuckled at the weirdness of his random thought. Shock kicked in immediately after. He ran to the nurses' station.

'Excuse me! Where is Zoe? The woman stabbed in the leg? Was she moved into another room?'

The young nurse sat back with eyes wide open. The tall man she was talking to turned and stared at Damien with clear annoyance. His mouth was open as he was ready to give Damien a piece of his mind. Yet it was a familiar voice that Damien heard.

'Sir! This is a hospital!' said the head nurse as she walked over. 'There will be no shouting here and please, police or not, you will respect the line!'

Just then did Damien notice the man next to him with his papers in hand. He turned his head and saw the two women standing a meter behind the man.

'I'm sorry,' he said toward them and then turned toward Voula, the obese head nurse with the thick-framed red glasses and the black hair in a beehive. 'This is a murder case, sister. I would think you would realize the word emergency. Where is Zoe Misiaouli? The victim in that room right there?'

Mrs. Voula rolled her eyes so far up; you could see only white behind her frames. 'Lieutenant, came to the side, please. Let the nurse do her job,' she said as she walked to the side of the counter. 'Zoe checked herself out, minutes after you left this morning.'

'Checked herself out? She was in no state to…'

Mrs. Voula raised her palm. 'I know. She wasn't even going to let us know. She stumbled down the hallway and one of the nurses stopped her. I went up to her and she asked to be discharged. I told her I would call her doctor. It was a bit hectic at that moment and by the time, the doctor swung by her room, to talk to her, she was gone. Vanished.'

Damien punched the counter. 'And you did not think to inform us?'

'Excuse me, Mr. Alpha Male banging on my counter, but we had no order to surveillance her. Where is the officer you lot have outside rooms of criminals in such cases? You said she was a victim. We treated her as any other patient.'

"Aaagh!' Damien raised his hands. 'Shit!' He quickly pulled his phone out of his right pocket. He brought it to his ear and walked away down the long corridor with the cheap art imitations hanging crookedly on its white walls.

'Good day to you, too, Mr. Sunshine,' Mrs. Voula remarked, shook her head, and returned to her loud, aging computer.

'This is Lieutenant Damien Levanti. I need an alert out for a Miss Zoe Misiaouli, age 24, description in file case CF 128-67. Airport and port, immediately.'

Damien walked outside and headed toward the only non-occupied bench. He sat down on the vibrant green wood and exhaled. 'You were blinded by her charm, fool. Think. Think, Damien. Why did she leave? Why did she lie about being hired by the daughter? Could it have been all planned?'

Damien closed his eyes. '*What details do not stick?*'

'The agency lies.'

'The empty photo frames.'

'Zoe never mentioning calling her roommate all the time in her story.'

His eyes opened wide, and he looked up at the clear sky.

'The nurses mentioning that she was quite clueless when they told her her stats and such…'

'Leo's blood in daughter's hair…'

His phone was still in his hand. He went to his recent calls and redialled.

'Hello?'

'It's me again.'

'Thanks for putting the phone down on me. I've been worried sick since you hung up. Zoe's phone is still switched off!'

'I'm sorry, Antigone. I did not mean to worry you. I can't share information with you, but I need a favor. For Zoe.'

'A favor?'

'Can you send me a photograph of Zoe?'

Damien heard a loud gasp. 'Oh my God! She's dead, isn't she?'

'A photograph, please. A clear view of her face. Send to this number, ASAP.'

Antigone found herself again, crying and pacing up and down her small kitchen due to the police Lieutenant hanging up on her. She picked up the energy drink she had opened and downed it in a matter of three seconds. She bit her nails as she tried to relax. She sat back on one of her wobbly (due to the girls' wrong set up) IKEA chairs and began to scroll though her phone's gallery. 'No, not that one... that one's dark... this one!' She stared at a smiling, bright, vibrant Zoe posing by the town's historic clock.

Damien smoked two cigarettes before his phone beeped. His legs shook as he sat on the bench contemplating on calling Antigone back. 'Why the heck is she taking so long?'

He quickly tapped on the app and opened the photograph as two swallows flew and danced joyfully above him. They had built their next in the corner formed by the hospital's main building and its adjacent cafeteria.

Damien leapt to his feet and cursed out loud startling people passing by and gaining disapproving looks by two mothers holding hands with their young offspring. Damien did not bother with apologies. Once again, he found himself running to his car with his phone glued to his ear.

'Anneta, its Damien. Listen we have got this all wrong!'

Anneta had never heard his voice break nor him speaking in such a high pitch. She ordered her co-workers to be quiet and even placed her hand above her vacant ear. 'Damien, what is wrong?'

'The woman in the hospital is not Zoe, the nurse. Zoe is the dead woman in her twenties we found in the house.'

'Then who was in the hospital?'

'The daughter! Alice! Get them to change the alert, now! Everywhere! Before she leaves the island!'

Chapter Nineteen

The next few hours were painful for Damien. His inner demons were having a field day, beating him up and ridiculing him for his mistake, for his failure to get over his weakness for a beautiful dame in distress and see the case clearly. Worst part is that the news had broken out nationwide and compared to the few local journalist who were outside the station the previous day, now dozens of news vans were lined up along the street and multiple crews had set up camp. The reporters were just as bad as his demons.

'So many dead and you had only two officers on the case?'

'Who was the detective so easily fooled?'

'Is this the level of competence our tax money deserves?'

'Do you not have any professional criminologist on board?'

'What did the coroner report? How did they all die?'

'Any word on the missing woman?'

'Is Alice considered a murderer?'

The tsunami of questions crushed upon the police captain who stood his ground. Standing steady on the stations top step, he answered all their questions swiftly and to the point.

Damien had had enough. He took a few steps back and left the scene. He felt of no use there and definitely was in no mood to answer any questions. Even though, he knew many officers were on duty there, he drove down to the port. He knew it was harder to escape through the airport as security was tight, but tourist ships offering excursions and especially smaller boats for hire was an easy way to escape.

As he parked in the car park cutting into the hill by the sea, he smiled as he saw quite a few police officers in their navy-blue uniforms carrying Alice's photograph and asking around. As he walked over, he spotted more on duty by the promenade checking people as they boarded. He also carried a headshot of Alice. Over a hundred were printed at the station as all officers were called in for the search. Damien jogged away from the main port and headed to the small bay by the main port. Smaller boats floated on the clear Ionian waters. Damien approached ageing sea-captains with long grey beards sitting by their boats. He walked up to everyone with a sign 'TO HIRE'. No one had ever seen Alice before. Half an hour later, he walked back to his car, dragging his feet, squinting his eyes as the bright sun showed no mercy. 'Great day to forget your sunglasses on your desk!'

Just then, his phone began to ring.

'Anneta? Please, tell me we have something. Anything!'

'A bank manager from the National Bank of Greece called. The main one down Independence Street. He said Alice was there this morning!'

'I'm five minutes away. See you there!'

Damien pushed down on all four window controls allowing the strong winds to invade his vehicle as he sped back into town. As the sun shone down on the town by the endless blue, Damien could not help but think of an old notion of his. 'A paradise should not have so many murders.' He turned into the avenue where the bank was located and added, 'or so much traffic.' Damien illegally parked upon the pavement outside the bank. His two back wheels occupied a part of a parking spot assigned for a person with a disability. He whispered a soft 'sorry' as he abandoned his vehicle. An apology aimed towards his inner guilt. He did try his best to keep out the spot, but the pavement was not easy to conquer with its many signs and metal bins.

Damien was the first one there. He ran up the marble steps to the tall columns of the biggest bank of the island. The original building was built by the Italians in 1840 before the islands became a part of the new modern Greek state. The bank was closed for the public, but most employees were still aside deeply preoccupied with their duties. A security guard buzzed Damien in after seeing his badge. 'Mr. Stephanopoulos is expecting you. His office is on the top floor. The big corner one on your right.'

Damien exited the elevator on the third floor. It was deserted as everyone had clocked off for the day. Damien went straight to the only person still in his office. The manager stood up from behind his grand desk as he saw through the glass wall, Damien walking up to his office.

'Sir, I am Lieutenant Damien Levante, the officer in charge of the case,' Damien said as he entered the office through the open door.

The manager ticked every cliché box possible for a

Greek man in charge of a major bank. An expensive dark blue suit covered a large round belly while a violet tie with silver stripes ran down his white shirt. His thinning hair encompassed multiple shades of grey as did his thick moustache. He spoke loudly and walked in a rather pompous manner as he moved out from behind his desk and approached Damien. His smile though was genuine, and he showed great willingness to help.

'Sit, Lieutenant,' he said and pointed to one of the two armchairs in the corner by the window. The manager sat in the other.

'Great view,' Damien could not resist commenting as he saw the town below running down to the endless blue of the Ionian that never ceased to amaze Damien. He could think of nothing more soothing, more relaxing, more beautiful than the sea on a fine clear day with a strong sun above.

'Yes, yes. Of course,' the manager said without even looking out. 'I called as soon as I saw the photo on my news feed. Mirela's daughter, Alice.'

'She was here you stated?'

'Yes. Come in around four hours or so ago. I was called down at twenty to nine exactly.'

'Why were you called down?'

'I am called down whenever a client wishes to open their safe deposit box. It takes two keys to open. I have the one and the client has the other. I make it my job to know all that own such security boxes.'

'And Alice opened such a box? Was it in her name?'

The manager nodded. 'Her mother is an old customer of ours. She came to us many years ago. I was not the manager back then, but I was the one that helped her with her inheritance and stocks left to her by Mrs. Thalia. Mrs. Mirela was really kind to me and after I went out of my way to help her out with everything, she spoke to the bank manager and that's when I got my very first promotion.'

'Why did you go out of your way, as you say, to help her?'

The manager scratched his knees and smiled. 'The noble answer would be that she was a sick woman, a weak widow and I felt sorry for her. She needed help filling in forms and getting the right documents ready. You can imagine the paperwork.'

'And the non-noble answer?'

'It was a four-million-euro case. I got lucky. It was the kind of case that would catch the eye of my superiors. I needed all to go well and the client to be happy. From then on, whenever she needed something, she called me. One day, a decade back, when the crisis hit the country, Mirela showed up accompanied by her daughter. She heard that in Cyprus, a bank shut down and deposits were confiscated. Only your first one hundred thousand were safe. That's when she asked for a safety box. I told her it wasn't as simple as taking money out of your account and putting it in a box. We couldn't move such sums without penalties and percentages being cut. That's when I thought of her daughter who was underage. We could put the deposit safe in her name and Mirela would give her the inheritance tax free. I promised to make sure that as much money as possible would physically end up in the safe rather than as a number in an unsafe account.' He paused to take a deep breath. 'Not that Mirela was fond of the idea. She did not want her daughter to have access to her cash. I told her that she wouldn't as Mirela would have the key.'

'And when Alice showed up today with the key, you did not ask any questions?'

The manager sat up straight. 'Of course, I did. She

brought me signed papers from her mother giving her... blessing let's say as the safe was in Alice's name anyway. She had every right to open it. Besides Mirela took a turn for the worst in recent years and is bed-ridden and even has early stages of Alzheimer's. I thought nothing of it. Alice said she was only going to take twenty thousand from the box as she needed to buy a new car. An SUV suitable for taking her mother to and from the doctors she said. She wanted it cash as she was buying from a local dealer, and he was giving her a better price if she paid in cash. I thought that was a pretty reasonable amount. I even told her to take a bit more as SUVs tend to cost a bit more than twenty and she should buy something better than one around that price.'

Damien exhaled loudly. 'And did you see her take out the cash?'

The manager tilted his head to the right and gently bit his lower lip. 'Err... no. We offer privacy to our customers when with their safes.'

Damien sighed. 'And how much exactly was in that box?'

'From my knowledge of the original transfers, a bit over two million...'

'Two million!'

A knock on the door caught their attention. Anneta stood side by side with a tall policeman. 'I see you got here before us, Lieutenant Levante. What did we miss?'

'Not much. This fine gentleman is going to show us footage from this morning. Fancy seeing our suspect walking out of here with a large bag containing roughly two million in cash?'

Chapter Twenty

The Heiress Case played well on the evening news. Alice's image was broadcast, and the unbelievable tale caught Greece's attention. Media in all its forms unravelled the story of murder and inheritance and all the mysteries left unanswered led to scrutiny over police handling. Damien was placed on a mandatory two-week leave after being filmed cursing at reporters following him as he walked his dog.

Damien had been a broken man for years. Now he was in shatters. He knew that Alice was no longer in Greece. How could she be? It had been days since the entire nation learnt her face. '*She could not be in hiding. She got out.*' Damien missed the only thing that kept him going. His job. He wasn't fired but it was the first time that he heard negative remarks on his professional skills. Not by a friend or a colleague, but by all the society eating up the juicy story. Damien did not bother with eating anymore. He was on a strict alcohol diet for five days straight.

It was on Friday morning when life took another swing at him. And it was the last, he was willing to take.

Jolie woke up and slurped away on the remaining water in her tin bowl. She then leapt onto the bed and with her paw, tried to wake up her master. He was unconscious, lost in deep slumber provided by Mr. Jack and Mr. Johnnie. She bit on the thin summer sheet and pulled in off him. He was completely naked. She placed both of her front paws on his back and pressed down. The bed squeaked but Damien remained silent. Her final weapon was her wet nose. She pressed in against his neck and with her tongue slightly out she journeyed up to his ear.

'For fuck's sake, Jolie! That's disgusting!' Damien pushed himself up and wiped the saliva hanging from his ear.

Jolie jumped off the bed, picked up her leash with her teeth and began dancing around. She dropped it by the door and barked loudly. The message was clear. 'Get up!'

'Give me five minutes, you raving lunatic.' Damien kept his promise. Toilet, clothes, frappe and ready to be out the door in exactly three-hundred seconds, much to Jolie's delight.

It took less than five minutes for Jolie to rush to her favorite spot in the field by the park and sit down to relieve herself.

'Fancy a walk around the park?' Damien asked and regretted having the free time to ask such a thing. He normally had to rush to work. As he was crossing the road, a tall lady with her chestnut hair locked under a red cap ran up to him.

'Lieutenant, can I have a word? I am with the Daily News and I would like your opinion…'

'Go away. I have nothing to say to any of you.'

She stood in front of him, blocking his way. 'Yes, but I

am writing a piece about Alice's life and as you are the only person she spoke to after the massacre, I was wondering…'

Damien raised his hands and asked her to back off. Jolie's leash fell from his hand and the dog ran to go to the park opposite. The screeching of the truck's tires made Damien jump and turn, just in time to see Jolie being knocked over. The truck could not stop in time and the Jolie went under the large front wheel. Damien shivered all over as he took small steps toward the pool of blood that painted the black asphalt. The van went back a meter, revealing the dead canine. People stopped to stare at the man lifting his bleeding dog and walking back to his apartment. Behind closed doors, Damien screamed and lay down beside his friend. He stroked her on her head and after many years, he cried. The old lady who lived on the ground floor and owned the small bakery Damien shopped from, saw the entire scene. With her hand upon her heart, she dialed the number to the police station and asked for Lieutenant Damien's partner.

Anneta arrived at his apartment an hour later. Damien was still on the floor with Jolie in his embrace when she knocked on the door. Weak, defeated, depressed, he got up and dragged his feet to the door.

Anneta's arms came through the open door and Damien found himself being hugged. He closed his eyes and rested on her shoulder. Anneta could not take hers off the poor animal that was severely wounded all over.

'There, there. Leave it all up to me. There is a pet cremation center just out of town. You go get cleaned and I will get my cousin to come with his pick-up truck. He will drive Jolie up there and I'll take you.'

Damien mumbled a thank you and walked into the bathroom.

Two hours later, he squeezed on Anneta's hand as he witnessed Jolie being rolled into the flames.

Damien sat quietly on the route back home, his eyes on the tall waves roaming the bay below. A group of divers preparing their gear caught his eye.

'Koror Island,' he whispered.

'Excuse me? What was that, Damien?'

'Nothing. Just take me home. I want to be alone, if you don't mind.'

'Of course.'

He placed his hand on her shoulder. 'I really appreciate everything you did today.' Anneta just nodded and kept her eyes on the country road that led back to town. 'I appreciate everything you have ever did for me. You're a good person, Anneta and an even better officer. Keep up the good work.'

Anneta did not realize at the time that that was Damien's goodbye.

Chapter Twenty-One

Two days. Forty-eight hours straight punishing his body and mind. Damien drunk himself to the verge of passing out. He downed his bottles of whiskey, curled up on his bed and shed tears for every loss in his life. Forty-eight hours and one minute, he stood up and shouted 'enough!' He picked up a large blue bin bag and started throwing the bottles in. The was the last time he wished to be numb. He could not go on like this, nor did he desire to. He craved a new beginning. A new life. A new Damien. Not the old *bundle of sorrow*.

He indulged in a lengthy shower, wore clean clothes, and pulled down his biggest suitcase from storage. It did not take him long to pack. Underwear, socks, jeans, trousers, t-shirts, and shirts were all thrown in the blue suitcase. He had no use of memorabilia. Nothing from the past. He wrote down a note to his landlady, put it in an envelope with his keys and next month's rent in a check.

He stepped outside into the sun and felt reborn. He was just in time for the bus. Final stop Corfu International Airport. Damien knew well that multiple flights were available to Athens. He bought a ticket on the next plane leaving and slept through the one-hour-something flight. At Athens airport, he headed to inquiries to organize the rest of his long journey. He booked a flight to Kuala Lumpur for the following morning. That gave him enough time to sit and write his resignation letter and email it to his captain. Fast food followed. As he dipped his burger in the pool of ketchup that he had created on the thin wrapping paper, he observed the people around him. A weird melting pot of anxiety and happiness. Joyful tourists arriving, happy Greeks returning from their holidays and ecstatic people reuniting after a long period of time. Yet many were rushing, stressed to find their flight. Others were arguing over extra luggage weight, the crying, tired kids, the expenses, the delays.

Could life offer you only happy moments? Would we appreciate them if it was not for the sad ones? Was it a utopia, a dream, a fantasy to believe he could leave it all behind and begin anew? Damien's thoughts taunted him. He hated doubts. He had a plan, and he was determined to go through with it to the very end.

He contemplated booking a room for the night at the hotel across the street. Its rooms looked spacious and quite luxurious from the photos on its website and the prices were not that hefty. Yet, Damien knew himself well. The armchairs in the lounge area suited him just fine.

After midnight, the hectic airport quieted down. Few people were moving around, and announcements became scarce. With his feet on his suitcase and his head on the comfortable red armchair, Damien drifted off to dream of new beginnings. And answers. He knew that her answer could ruin his plan on a new start. His moral police compass needed a decent closure.

Damien had never travelled much. Never outside of Europe and definitely had never taken four flights in two days. Corfu to Athens, Athens to Kuala Lumpur, Kuala Lumpur to Manila and then Manila to Palau.

With relief, he exited the small airport in Palau and let the heat attack his body after being in air conditioning for the last forty hours. The air carried the scent of the sea and made the Greek islander smile. He walked over to the first taxi in the long line of cabs.

The taxi driver towered him -and Damien was considered tall, at least for a Greek man- as he flicked his cigarette away and approached with a smile. 'Welcome, buddy. Need a ride?' he asked in a distinct accent. Almost singing out the words. A loud, happy accent resembling more of an American accent than the British one Damien was accustomed with due to the half a million of Brits that visited his island every year.

'Good morning. Yes, I need a ride to Koror.'

The large man picked up his luggage with ease and Damien sat in the back seat as Ariihau as he later introduced himself, placed his suitcase in the back. The vehicle shook as he sat down in the driver's seat and stepped on the gas.

'So where are you from, stranger?'

'Greece.'

Ariihau's eyes opened wide. 'Never met a Greek before, but I know much about your country. Land of democracy and the ancient Gods. So many words we use that are Greek. I would love to visit one day.'

It seemed chatty taxi drivers were a universal rule. At least on islands. Damien nodded. 'Yes, definitely worth it.'

'So, what's your name and what does it mean? Greek

names always have meaning, right? Same with us. I'm Ariihau which means king of peace.'

'Great name. That's what we are all looking for. Some peace.'

'Well said, stranger.'

'I'm Damien which means to tame, to conquer, to overcome.'

'Sounds like you're on a mission to achieve peace,' the driver said as he turned onto the main road. 'Look there's our famous bridge ahead. It connects us to the island of Koror. It's called the Japan-Palau friendship bridge, built after World War two.

As the vehicle crossed the tall, 400-meter bridge, the driver asked, 'so, what hotel are we heading to?'

'Err, none really. Take me to the benches along Long beach.'

Ariihau looked in his rear-view mirror. 'Not judging or anything, man, we are a pretty safe country but camping out on a bench is not safe for your stuff. Besides, the night bugs will eat you alive.'

Damien smiled. 'I am meeting up with a friend.'

'Oh, I see.'

The last five minutes of the twenty-minute drive consisted of Damien gazing out the window as Ariihau acted as a tour guide.

'What a beautiful place. A paradise,' Damien commented as he saw the clear waters running up to sandy beaches. Wooden houses lost in greenery were scattered all around while the main street consisted of hotels, bars, and shops.

The vehicle came to a halt under a bent palm tree.

'Thank you,' Damien said as he paid the driver by card.

'Enjoy your stay.' Ariihau kept his eyes on the peculiar

visitor without a place to stay and watched him put on his dark shades as he stepped into the bright sun, rolling his suitcase behind him, heading over to the beach.

'Man doing some crazy shit? Has to be for a woman,' Ariihau mumbled as he reversed the car. He had to head back to the airport. 'Money does not grow on trees,' he mimicked his grandma's voice as he sped away.

Damien stopped by the grass and took his time to take the scenery in. A mile-long sandy beach spread out in front of him. Clear waters painted generously with multiple shades of blue crashed upon the white sand. The wind made the palm trees sing as the waves provided the bass to their song. Carefree locals and tourists blended into the paradise as they strolled along barefoot in their swimwear.

The sky above reminded him of home. A generous mighty fireball dominating an azure cloudless sky. 'Home!' He found himself mocking the word. He looked around and spotted the green benches Alice had talked about. None of their occupants though were Alice. Damien sat down on the only one that was empty. He sat and as he leaned back, fear kicked in. '*What a fool you are, Damien! Did you really expect her to be sitting here? She could be anywhere on the planet! Heck, she could be hiding out in a cottage in Corfu, for all you know. Real life, man. Not some Notting Hill, Notebook love story.*'

Then, he smiled, remembering how he was not going to be a slave of his thoughts any more. A chilled, sober, better version of himself was his goal. Alice or no Alice. '*Besides, she could be diving as we speak or by the pool of her luxury hotel,*' he encouraged himself.

Hours came and went as Damien people-watched and kept his mind busy with making up background stories about them and imagining crimes they were capable of. His game might have kept his brain preoccupied, yet his stomach had a mind of its own. It grumbled in retaliation of being ignored. Damien knew it was time for a walk to the bakery shop across the narrow road. 'At least, its outside tables have a view of the benches.'

As he pushed back the door and the little bell announced his arrival, a strong scent of cinnamon attacked his nostrils. A rich array of goods filled his view and Damien found himself spoilt for choice. Damien was never one for trying exotic food. He played it safe, opting for a sausage roll and a cinnamon bun. As he read the prices in dollars, the young man behind the register welcomed him. After receiving his change, Damien asked 'where is the cheapest place to stay, last minute without a reservation? Nothing fancy. Simple stuff that won't break the bank.'

A wide smile spread upon the youth as he pointed to a sign to his left. ROOMS FOR RENT. 'Mum has a couple of rooms left; I think. Plain, but clean and cheap and you can't beat us for location. They are all behind the bakery and my dad's restaurant next door.'

Damien tried to waste as little time as possible as he checked in, paid for two nights, threw his luggage on the single bed, and rushed back outside, beverage and pastries in hand. No one on the benches was Alice. He sat down to enjoy his lunch. And wait. He waited until the sun went down and the magical place lit up with a plethora of bright colorful lights under the starry night.

He walked around until his heart told him to give up the search. He resisted showing strangers her picture on his phone. That was not the way. He wanted to meet her as Damien, the civilian not Levante, the Lieutenant.

The next day found him in his newly bought red swimming shorts walking towards a wooden booth promoting scuba diving lessons. He did not make it that far. He froze on the spot. Alice sat on the bench by the booth preparing her diving equipment. He took in the deepest breath of his life as he began to walk up to her. He had practised his lines many times during his flights yet sweat ran down the back of his neck as he approached the woman checking her oxygen tank.

That is when she raised her eyes.

Alice thought that after *that* night, nothing would surprise her ever again. She placed her hand upon her heart as she feared it would burst out of her chest. '*Relax. He can't arrest you here. Scream for help if you must.*' Then, she noticed the red shorts and the sunglasses in his hair. Her words. Her description. He was smiling. She exhaled, dropped everything she was holding and stood up. '*He remembered.*'

Damien stopped a couple of meters from her. The two stared at each other and neither spoke for what seemed an eternity.

'Hi,' he mastered.

'Well, this is a surprise. Nice shorts.'

Damien chuckled. 'I can't believe you are here.'

'I can't believe *you* are here! If you open a dictionary and look up surreal, there will be a photo of this very moment.'

'When I first left Greece, it seemed so logical. Yesterday, I realized what a fool I had been and how random it would be for you to actually be here. The odds of winning the lottery.'

'And yet, here we stand.'

'Indeed.'

Alice stroked her left arm and looked down at her feet. 'You're too relaxed to be here to arrest me.'

'Indeed, again.'

'So…'

'I'm here for closure to the last chapter of my old life.'

'Closure?'

Damien placed both his hands behind his head. 'I need the true story. I need to know if...' His arms fell to his sides. He looked away. The ocean was always comforting, soothing, a remedy for tortured souls.

'If?'

'Let's stick to the closure part first.' He smiled. 'Shall we sit? You owe me another story. One containing the truth this time.'

Alice sat down facing the sea, and Damien sat down beside her this time.

'I told you the truth the first time.'

'Come on. You played me for a fool once.'

Alice shook her head, and a string of flame red hair escaped her bun. She placed her hand upon his. 'I'm sorry you felt that way. That was never my intention. I told you exactly what you asked for. Zoe's story. Zoe's truth. Everything I told you happened for real. I told you everything that happened to her.'

'And how would you know such details?'

'Cameras. My mum had a few hidden around the house. She loved spying on the cleaners and visitors. On us, her kids. All connected to her phone. I also linked my phone to them before Zoe arrived. She spoke every night to her roommate and retold her entire day. From her meals to her chores, to her different encounters.' She turned to face him. 'Damien, I never lied to you.'

'Only about who you were.'

'I would not be able to escape otherwise.'

'Escape? This was not your plan to get the millions from the bank?'

'You think three people dead was my plan? You pin me for such a cruel ruthless person?'

Damien placed his elbows on his knees and lowered his head into his hands. 'I think you owe me another story. Your side.'

'And at the end you will decide?'

'Decide what?'

'If you want to stay here with me.'

Damien found himself lost for words and gazing into her calm eyes. 'I'm I such an open book?' he finally managed to mutter.

'I think we both felt the same spark back in that hospital room. And I don't believe that would you venture around the world just to get closure. You desire a new beginning as much as me. But your moral compass holds you back. If I am guilty of a crime, of murder, you can't be with me, right?'

Damien laughed out of awkwardness. 'You seriously have me figured out. Case solved.'

'I will not ask you for a leap of faith. I will be square with you. You deserve to know that I never planned harm on Zoe or her boyfriend. This is not how I wished for events to play out.'

Damien moved closer to her. He looked her straight in the eye. 'All I want to know is who I am mending my heart for.'

Alice placed her hand over her mouth and slowly turned her attention to the travelling waves, riding through the bay. 'I have never known love before. I have lived a pretty miserable existence. I don't know what you have uncovered about my mother, but she was a monster. A body without a heart or soul. She murdered her aunt for that house and managed to get everyone else cut out of their inheritance. Once, she even mentioned how she pushed her cousin, Evagoras out of the window and made his wife believe it was suicide. Wicked being. My...' She paused to swallow the lump blocking her words. Damien knew well from years of interrogations to never interrupt a speaking, bare-it-all, confessionist. 'My brother and I grew up afraid of her. She would use her illness to force us to do what ever she wanted. We grew up with guilt and in terror. Any sort of disobedience was punished harshly. I was only eight when she locked me in the basement for four days straight. When she was a smoker, she would put them out on my brother's back for a whole month when she found a porn movie in his room. He was like thirteen at the time. We never socialized with anyone but between us. No one spoke to us as the entire village hated us and did not let their kids be friends with us. Mum loved pranks and stealing so you can imagine how popular she was with the local folk. She ventured out at nights and stole anything that she knew mattered to someone. Just to cause pain. For fun! You know, the mansion has secret passages and she used them to scare the cleaners or nurses. Remember the doorbell from Zoe's tale? She had a button that set it off in her drawer.' Alice was shaking as she spoke, and tears were allowed to run free. 'Anyway,' she said and pushed some renegade hairs back behind her ear. 'Long story, short and all, our studies saved us. I left for Athens and a couple of years later, Theodore left the island, too. Life sucked as the rich bitch sent us zero money. It was her way to force us back. But we managed. We had to work while our fellow students partied and mingled. But we were free. I stayed in Athens even after I got my degree. I lied that I was going to do a master's degree and then go for my PHD. She would have cut me out of her will if she knew that I was lying. She wanted us close to torture us. Our inheritance was her weapon. It wasn't that I craved her fortune, but money frees you, you know? She was sick. After the childhood that I had, I knew that I had to be strong. Strong until she died and then I would be free. Free to journey out of Greece. To start a family and be nothing like her.' A slight cough stopped her. Alice looked at Damien. She had his full attention, yet he remained silent. She decided to continue without asking him for his thoughts. 'As she got older, she started to lose it even more. Forgetting gave her another firearm to attack with. She said and did whatever she wanted and then pretended to not remember. One day, a couple of months back, she called me and demanded that I come stay with her for the weekend. She sounded all nice over the phone and mentioned that she paid for a plane ticket for me. I fell right into her trap. At home, she tells me to have a shower and dress with what she had bought me. A silky, revealing black dress and some slutty high heels. God knows where she ordered them from. We had a guest over for dinner. An old man with a huge belly who smoked cigars in the house. She tells me that he is *really* rich and owns many businesses. It was a set up. She tells me that she has fixed me up an arranged marriage. That the man would take her stocks and businesses to new highs. She basically wanted to sell me off. I refused. During drinks after dinner, I felt drowsy. Weak. Disoriented. She had the man dance with me. I could feel his hands all over me, yet I could not stop him. They took me to the guest room on the ground floor. My mum undressed me, lay me on the bed and told the man to have fun. I woke up sore and ashamed realizing that my own mother drugged me. The door was locked. She denied letting me go until I came to my senses and agreed to marry the multi-millionaire. I called my brother to come save me.'

Alice finally wiped her eyes. 'It was all my fault. I should never had asked him to come save me. I am the reason he snuck into the house the following night. She thought it was a burglar and stabbed him in the dark. His face must have shocked her to her core as the following morning when she heard me screaming for release, she opened my door and acted as if nothing had happened. She remembered nothing about my ordeal. She was all like, oh, dear, you came to visit, that's sweet. I saw the blood on her hands. I investigated the house and found my poor baby brother. Headless! I knew it was her. She chopped off his head as to not see who she killed. By the way, I believe his head is in the old well behind the shed at the edge of the property. I searched all around the house. If there is a way for you to inform the authorities to check, please do. My brother deserves to be buried whole.' She choked on her words. She took her time to take in two slow deep breaths, before wiping her eyes. 'Anyway, I confronted my mother and shouted and screamed in fury, and she just stared at me. I dragged her down to the basement and I made her remember. I told her that I was calling the police. She smiled that sinister smile of hers. God, I hated that smile. She said, go ahead. Call them. I remember nothing, I will say. She said she would imply that I killed him as I was always jealous of him and wished to be her sole heir. She laughed and said that she would rather leave her fortune to a dog shelter than to me. Help the four-legged bitches rather than the two-legged one that wants to have her locked up. She called the university and told them that Theodore was quitting their shitty institution and then she locked the basement up. I knew I had to do something, but I knew that her punishment could not mean me going to prison. I wanted her out the picture and me with my inheritance and a new life. So, after a few weeks when the nurse that visited her twice a week quit, I came up with a plan. I made up the whole agency story and told my mum, it is really cheap to have a live-in nurse and went through ads to find the most inexperienced nurse. I read their resumes and I chose one without a family. My plan was to stay near-by at a farmhouse I rented and mix up my mum's pills every night. I knew a nurse right out of school wouldn't know each of her pills by colour. I hoped it would make my mum sick and hopefully slowly kill her. She was on her way out anyway. It was the pills keeping her alive. I knew she would refuse to go to the hospital. I never wished for Zoe to get the blame. The worst would be a case of malpractice. That's why I looked for one without a family. So there would be no one to be in pain if she did do a bit of time. I never, in a million years, imagined that she would bring her married lover over and set off my mother's killing instincts. I saw my mum chop off the man's hand from the cameras and I started running through the fields to get over there. I wanted to protect them. Help them. By the time, I got there, Leo was dead, and my mum was taking her last breaths. Zoe gave me no time to explain. She heard me call Mirela, mum and that was it. She lunged at me and stabbed me in the leg. She was scared shitless and in a state of panic. She raised the knife to stab me again and that's when I fought for my life. You must believe me, Damien. It was self-defense. I am not a bad person. Just a hurt one. One wishing to escape. And there was the opportunity. I did not want to risk jail time. I had been locked up my entire life. No more. With my mother's bank key in my underwear, I took Zoe's wallet with her ID and threw it in the gap between the walls, along with any photos of me and limped out to you saying I was Zoe, the nurse. To be honest, it was all so ludicrous, I never expected it to work. But God or the universe or whoever, gave me a break. I am here, with my millions and now, the handsome man with the kind eyes that saved me, is here, too.' She stroked his cheek.

'I believe you.'

Three words. That's all it took. That was all that she needed to hear. She lay her head upon his shoulder and stayed there gazing out at the sunrays dancing upon foaming waves.

'How did you get out of Greece?'

'Detective mind cannot rest, huh? I took a fishing boat to Turkey's deserted shores. Paid a guy a hefty price for his gas and his silence. In Turkey, I took an Uber under a different account to a private airfield. One that does not check its client's luggage or identities. In the Philippines, I got a boat again out to here. Here I can be myself again. No Interpol allowed here. I rent a villa nearby. I'm thinking of buying it if someone would be interested in moving in with me.'

'A new beginning, huh?'

'Isn't that what we both wish for? And who is to say that life must be hard and complicated and tiring? We make our own luck from now on. A stress-free, terror-free, hurt-free life by the beach. Away from the cruelness and the wickedness of the world.'

'Kavafis says we carry our *town* inside us wherever we may go. There's no escaping ourselves, our weaknesses, our Achilles' heels that creep up and screw us over.'

Alice shook her head. 'I disagree with the great poet. Circumstances make us react. Action and reaction. New surroundings, new experiment, new results. And what's with all the focus on his bloody heel? Achilles was a demi-God and out of all his glory we focus there? Sorry, but no. I will no longer be a victim. I made it here. And here I will thrive.

The past has happened. I'd rather not think about it anymore. Let's write our own story from now on. We are two people that won the lottery right before our honeymoon and now that we are here and falling in love with the place, I am asking you to stay here forever. That will be our story.'

Damien tapped his fingers on the picnic table in front of the bench. 'I'll move in with you on one condition though.'

Alice sat up straight. 'Which is?'

'We are getting a dog.'

Alice laughed and placed her hands upon his face. 'Let's get two.'

Their first kiss felt liberating. A signal for things yet to come. A sign of repaired hearts and freedom acquired.

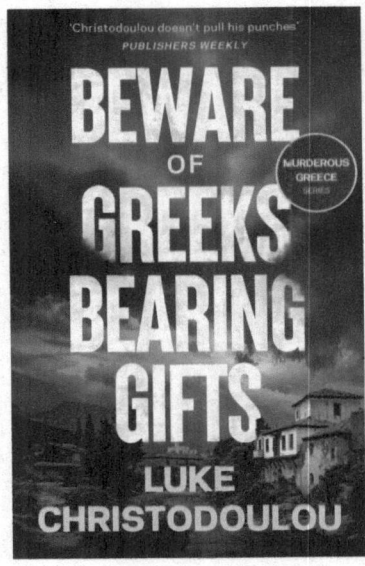

vinci-books.com/BewareOfGreeks

Grief brought her to Greece. What she found was far worse.

After her son's death, Susan travels with her family to her husband's ancestral mansion in Greece—hoping for healing, finding horror instead. As grief turns to dread, the house's dark past awakens, and Susan must confront something far deadlier than sorrow.

Turn the page for a free preview…

Beware of Greeks Bearing Gifts: Chapter One

PARGA, GREECE

Spring, 1913

Iphigenia stood by the open window, allowing the fresh sea air to rush into her small cottage. It carried the sweet smell of blossoming Greek flowers mingled up with the sharp salty scent of the Ionian Sea. The stone-paved streets below welcomed hundreds of joyful Greeks as they celebrated their union with the free state of Greece. Greece had emerged victorious from the Balkan War, and Ottoman rule came to an end after centuries of harsh occupation.

Iphigenia could not care less.

She slammed the blue wooden shutters, fastened the rusty lock, and slid down the old, decaying wall. Curled up on the cold floor, she gazed around the dark room. The two empty beds before her pierced her soul. Her handsome twin boys, both dead in the war. She carried them inside her for nine months and proudly raised them for eighteen years, and one letter from the front changed all that.

She was no longer a mother.

Iphigenia did not believe in crying. She cursed God and pushed herself up from the wooden ground. She dragged her feet out of their room and stood in the hallway. From the ajar door creaking in the spring breeze, she witnessed her husband sobbing in his armchair, an empty vessel of the man she once knew. Two months had passed since their boys' passing to the other world, and her husband had not left the house.

'You need to go tend to the land,' she had urged him.

'Why? Who will inherit us, Effie? Who?'

'We need to eat, and frankly, we need to move on. Life is for the living...'

'I'm already dead. I have no reason to be alive.'

Iphigenia closed her eyes and sighed deeply. She quivered her head to shake away the memories of his words. She turned around, picked up her knitted jacket, and rushed out of the house. She wrapped her hazelnut hair inside her purple scarf as she walked by her neglected garden, and with her eyes lowered, she made her way through the ecstatic crowds dancing the evening away. Shorter than most, she moved through them, avoiding eye contact. Iphigenia headed away from the village's center; her eyes were set on the restless sea opposite. A row of rocky islands stood proudly in the cool waters of Parga. Saint Mary's chapel stood alone on the largest of the isles that nested in the small bay.

The planks of the dock squeaked as Iphigenia made her way toward her uncle's fishing boat. Born upon a ship to a family of fishermen, Iphigenia had no trouble untying nautical knots and releasing the boat from its chains. Both were soon free upon the short-lived waves of Parga Bay. With her hands firmly gripped around the paddles, she steered the small boat to the shore of the church-owned island.

Father Gregory stood behind the church's colored window, admiring the will of the woman with whom he grew up with. His teeth travelled along his thin lips as he scratched his left eyebrow. '*Well, well. What has the Lord have in store for me on this glorious day?*'

He opened the wooden door and rushed down the dirt path leading to the rocks that served as the islet's dock. He nodded to Iphigenia as he stepped in the shallow waters to help bring her boat nearer to shore. He offered his hand, and Iphigenia's icy hand grabbed hold of him, and as many times before, she jumped to land.

'Good evening, Father.'

'Went looking for me at St. Nicholas?' he replied and coughed.

Iphigenia wiped her hands on her black dress; the dirt on her hands left behind lines of mud as it blended with the droplets offered by the splashing of the Ionian. 'I know you well. You're not one for much commotion. Also, you're not one to miss a spring sunset from Saint Mary's island. One look at the clear sky above, and I did not even bother to go look for you at your church.'

Father Gregory's thick beard was lifted by a sincere wide smile.

'Come in,' he said and sauntered back up the path. 'What is on your mind?' he asked as he stood by the door, waiting for her to enter the high-ceilinged church. Iphigenia fought back tears as she did the sign of the cross upon her body and made her way to the first row of wooden stools. 'Must be hard to find joy in our liberation, but you must rest assured that your boys are by our creator's side. Jesus once said ...'

'It's not my boys that I worry about, Father. It's Giorgo,' she interrupted him.

Father Gregory sat down by her side. He placed his hand on her trembling fingers. Iphigenia took a deep breath and sighed. 'I think he is going to do something crazy. I think he is going to take his own life. He will not listen to me. I feel his demons lingering in our house, in his head. You must talk to him!'

The following day, the bright Mediterranean sun found Greece nearly double in size. White smiles glowed on people's olive-skinned faces. Freedom, that once-elusive dream, was theirs to relish and savor. Tears fell from Father Gregory's green eyes as he praised Jesus for the euphoria of the people in his town. He ambled uphill through stone cottages and wished a good morning to all that greeted him. Children's laughter filled the air as they ran by him waving Greek flags. Soon, Father Gregory was leaning on the rusty gate of Iphigenia's home. He heard her shout out to her husband. 'Giorgo, I'm off to my aunt's.'

Iphigenia forced a smile as she nodded to him. 'Don't worry,' he managed to say as she sprinted off down the street. Father Gregory closed the gate behind him and paused to enjoy two merry swallows building their nest in the corner above the front door. He never married. He never truly understood why. Every time his parents mentioned a good Christian girl to him, he would come up with an array of excuses. Now, at thirty-seven, with his parents deceased and Greece a free country, he felt lonelier than ever.

'Good morning, Giorgo,' he said in a cheery voice as he popped his head through the open front door.

'What's so good about it?'

Father Gregory swallowed the lump forming inside his throat and entered the gloomy living room. The stuffy air housed the smoke from Giorgo's cigarettes, and the closed shutters blocked out the singing from the spring birds outside. He took out his Bible and sat by the sad man's side. He opened the Good Book. Nehemiah 8:10.

Beware of Greeks Bearing
Gifts: Chapter Two

Iphigenia felt the first sun rays of the day dance upon her
pale face. She pushed back locks of tangled hair from her
forehead and stretched her arms. Startled, she opened her
eyes and sat up. She was alone in bed. Giorgo never awoke
before her.

'Giorgo?'

Silence.

'Giorgo?' She raised her voice as her feet landed on the
wooden floor. Living room, kitchen, boys' room. She was
home alone. On her bare tiptoes, she leaned outside of the
bedroom window and called out her husband's name once
more.

'Lost your man, Effie?' her neighbor asked, poking her
head through the sheets she had just hung up to dry in her
narrow back yard.

'Seems so, Helena.' A faint smile spread along her tired
face. 'Could it be?'

She rushed back into her bedroom to dress. Maintaining

the same speed, Iphigenia exited her cottage and hastily set off for their land. Above, the sun painted the flock of innocent-looking clouds gathering in the blue sky. The long dirt road seemed longer to her as she paused by a stubborn olive tree growing out of a rocky surface, trying to catch her breath.

'Good morning, Iphigenia,' Jacob, the cheery farmer, called out. 'Off to your vineyard?' he asked; hints of sorrow came tangled in his words. He dared not mention the neglected fruit trees and the dying —most likely already corpses- vegetables. It had been months since he saw anyone on their land.

'Good day to you too, sir. Yes. I'm off to meet Giorgo.'

A wide smile lifted the farmer's thick mustache. 'Giorgo is back? That's great. Early as always, huh? I did not see him pass by.'

Iphigenia replied with a short-lived smile and a quick nod and continued down the road as the morning breeze circled her, raising clouds of dust around her running feet. Iphigenia stopped by the open gate and made her way through overgrown weeds, wild orchids, and sweet-smelling daffodils. The wind grew stronger as she entered the shadows of the rows of fruit trees. A gust swept the cold sweat forming on the back of her neck. Iphigenia froze. Like an ancient statue of a Greek Goddess she stood still, not moving a single muscle. Her eyes were fixed on the lifeless man hanging from a tall carob tree in the distance. His feet swung two feet from the ground, and his head lay on his right shoulder. She took a few steps forward, exhaling deeply. Her eyes followed the rope from the snapped neck up to the thick branch. More steps forward. An old wooden stool lay on the dry ground. She moved sideways, her eyes watering up. The face of the man she married at the tender age of seventeen. The blue eyes she once found herself getting lost in, now scared her. Two hollow, blood-red eyes, wide open, decorated a face of shock. Crimson saliva snake-lined from the corners of his purple-blue mouth. Iphigenia sat down in the dirt opposite his swinging corpse. She closed her eyes and let her senses travel around her land. The flowery aroma of spring would soon be ruined by the odoriferous, putrid smell of a dead body. The songs of the choirs of April's birds would soon be covered by her mother-in-law's loud cries.

Minutes passed before she placed her pale hands on the ground and lifted her body and spirit up. Emotionless, she stumbled out back onto the road and walked up to Jacob.

'Hey again! How's Giorgo doing?'

'He's dead,' she said and bit her bottom lip. 'I... I can't...' she stuttered as she sat down. 'Please go tell his brother,' she managed to say in one breath of a sentence before fainting in front of the shocked farmer.

Two days later, she would faint again. This time in Father Gregory's arms as he held her a foot away from her husband's final resting ground. The sky, even though spring, dressed for the occasion. Dark grey clouds roamed above the crowd crying as four men lowered the wooden coffin into the ground. Iphigenia knelt in the soft soil. Her fingers ran through the dirt. She raised her fist above the hole and watched as the casket settled six feet below. Her right arm trembled violently; her fingers were clenched into a fist, holding prisoner the earth inside. She shook her head. 'I can't...'

Father Gregory took a step forward and knelt by her side. 'Effie, you have to say goodbye. It's time for ...'

Thunder covered his last words. Iphigenia opened her fist, watched as crumbs of dirt dived down to Giorgo, and just as the first drops plummeted from the sky, she fainted into Father Gregory's arms.

Beware of Greeks Bearing Gifts: Chapter Three

LONDON, UK

Spring, 2010

Susan stared at her phone's screen as she sat alone on her old brown sofa in the attic of her three-bedroom home. Her teary eyes gazed at the four-year-old's lifeless little body, lying face down in the golden sand as the Aegean Sea washed him out on the Turkish coast. The news hit too close to home for her to handle.

Five months had passed since she last saw a child's body.

Her little Eugene would have been two if alive. Tears formed rivulets on her cold pale cheeks as she closed her eyes. She relived the moment often. She stood above her boy's cot and looked into his still eyes. She screamed frantically animal-like cries as she picked him up and shook his little body. He was cold and a sickly shade of white. Blood no longer ran through his veins. His tiny heart no longer gave a beat.

'Mum? Mum?'

Her teenaged daughter's calling pulled her out of the

nightmare. Her trembling arm reached out and flicked on the lights, scaring the darkness and the nightmare world away. She wiped her eyes and swallowed the lump in her throat. 'Yes, dear?'

'Where's my black jacket? I left it in the hallway and ...'

'In its place, Sophia.'

Silence.

'Your wardrobe!' Susan continued.

'Thanks, Mum. You're the best. See you later!'

Loud steps echoed toward Susan as she pictured Sophia running down the stairs, leaping them two-by-two. 'Why do I bother with the news? It's just all doom and gloom, doom and gloom,' Susan mumbled as she dropped her phone on the sofa and stood up, rubbing her aching lower back. 'Yeah, the bloody forties are the new twenties. Woo-fucking-hoo!'

Her bare feet slipped into her warm moccasins as she kneaded her neck and carelessly fixed her hair. 'It's seven o'clock already,' she said in one breath and made her way down to her modern rustic kitchen. Susan always had an eye and a heart for home design. Before having her four children, nothing could please her more than shop-hopping to find the perfect wooden counter or the cushion she had envisioned for a client's living room. She quit her job two days before Eugene's funeral. Andrew had held her in his strong arms and looked straight into her blue eyes while stroking her golden locks. 'You can't quit. You love your job. Psychologists say we must keep our minds busy at such times...' He began to recite some *bullshit* -as Susan referred to it- he had read online. 'The world is grey and cold and awful and hostile. My eyes are incapable of seeing color. How will I set up a home? I am an empty vessel,' she drunkenly replied.

The crackling of the sausages brought her focus back to the meal she was preparing. Susan poked them with the fork in her hand and rolled them over. Her eyes watched the boiling oil furiously roaming the black pan. She brought her palm above it; the heat attacked her skin. 'I need to feel,' she whispered, and she gradually lowered her hand toward the deep-frying pan.

The loud buzzing of her doorbell made her jump. She took a clumsy step back and breathed heavily. '*Get a grip, Susan!*'

The front door banged against its door stopper as its hinges retaliated to the force used by her son, Christopher. The fair-haired boy kicked off his shoes and threw his jacket in the direction of the metal coat rack. He missed. His sister, Maya, wobbled in behind him, a happy grin permanently occupying her round face. Andrew followed, shaking his head at the sight of the pair of shoes and the sports jacket that ruined the catalogue-picture-perfect tidiness of his home. It did not take much to awaken his OCD.

'Why do you always ring the doorbell when you have keys?'

'Hey, Ma! What's for dinner?' Christopher asked, ignoring her complaint.

Susan forced a large smile across her tired face. She stroked her son's hair and kissed his forehead. 'You're in high spirits.'

'I broke my personal record today. Fifty-six seconds!'

Susan hugged her ecstatic youth. 'That's amazing. Well done, Christopher!'

Christopher pulled out a wooden chair with aluminum tips and dramatically fell back on it. 'You didn't answer my question though.'

'Sausages, cabbage and chips. Your favorite!'

Susan felt two little arms wrapped around her right leg. 'Chips!' her three-year-old daughter repeated.

'Well hello, my baby. How was your day?'

Maya replied with a dance. She tip-toed the length of the kitchen, twirling her body around while her hair swirled, covering her face.

'I'll take that as a good sign,' Susan commented, her eyes on her husband walking in with Christopher's jacket and shoes. He threw them all on his son's lap. 'This' -he waved his arms three-hundred and sixty degrees- 'is not a pigsty. Go put them in your room.'

Christopher rolled his eyes but did not speak. He arched his back and dragged his feet past his parents.

'And wash your hands,' his mother added, while accepting a gentle kiss on her cheek. 'Where's Sophia?' Andrew asked as he remained close to her, rubbing her back. Susan remained still. 'At Katie's, down the road. She will eat there and be home later.'

'Great. I have news for you. *Just you.*'

Twenty-five minutes later, they both stood by the open dish-washer. Susan had tried to read her husband's enigmatic expression during dinner, and after various thoughts came alive in her head, she gave up on her personal guessing game and waited to hear his news. The hot water fell on her hands as she wiped the plates, keeping her warm from the cold air invading through the slightly opened window. The thin white curtains swayed to the rhythm of the wind, revealing the breeze growing in strength. As she handed the first plate to Andrew, droplets of icy water splashed against the glass.

'My mum has Alzheimer's.'

Susan continued pushing away a blob of ketchup. 'Thought you said you had news. As in something *new* to tell me.' She turned to his direction. 'Oh, no. *You* are starting to forget, *too!*' she joked, opening her eyes widely.

Andrew hid his annoyance and laughed. It was not often that he saw his once joyous and bubbly wife in high spirits. 'I spoke to the nursing home today. They called about some change in their payment methods, and I got an update on her health. She's getting worse. It seems to be all downhill from now on.'

'Poor Penelope. She used to be so... so vibrant, you know?'

Andrew nodded as he shut the window, taking in a deep breath of fresh air. 'It got me thinking...'

'You want to go to Greece to see her?'

Andrew bit his bottom lip and stared straight at her. Susan watched his thumbs play around with his fingers. 'Go on, spit it out.'

'I wanna us all to go. For the entire summer...'

Susan dropped the knife she was wiping into the soapy pool of the sink. Andrew never understood why she washed the dishes so well if she was going to place them in the dishwasher anyway.

'The *entire* summer?'

'Think about it,' Andrew said, raising his voice. Susan saw the spark in his round eyes come to life.

'Oh, God. Another one of his project ideas.'

'My mum inherited her grandma's old mansion. It stands on a great piece of land. We go for the summer, stay in the place, visit my mother and draw up plans to renovate the place. We are an amazing team. Projects are what we do best. Architect and designer superpower!'

'That doesn't even make sense.'

Andrew lowered his raised arms and placed his hands on her shoulders. 'I can only think of benefits. Others would give an arm and a leg for a summer in paradise, in Greece. The sun, the sea, the air... it will do us all good. My half-Greek kids should know more than a simple kalimera and efcharisto. We need this as a family. And you need to work, to design. And, I'll get to spend my mother's dying days by her side...'

'Nice play, Mr. Fotopoulos.'

Andrew chuckled and scratched the back of his neck. 'And, think about it. Greece's economy is finally on the rise again. Prices are going up. That mansion will one day be ours. Ours to sell. This could be two new cars for us. And all college expenses for all three of them. And all our future holidays.'

'What a wonderful future you paint. For all *five of us*. While *one of us* was placed in a small wooden box and thrown into the cold winter ground...'

Andrew pulled her into his arms and squeezed her upon his heavily breathing chest. 'I miss him, too. Every single day. I close my eyes, and there he is. His cheeky smile, and his shiny eyes. His uncontrollable laughter echoes in my ears. But we owe to our living kids, to our marriage, and to our mental health to do something. Anything! This is our home. Not a mausoleum.'

'And yet, you want to escape it.'

Grab your copy...
vinci-books.com/BewareOfGreeks

About the Author

Luke Christodoulou is an Amazon bestselling author, a poet and an English teacher (MA Applied Linguistics - University of Birmingham). He is also a coffee-movie-book-Nutella lover.

His first book, *The Olympus Killer* (#1 Bestseller - Thrillers), was released in April, 2014. The book was voted Book of the Month for May on Goodreads (Psychological Thrillers). The book continued to be a fan favorite on Goodreads and was voted BOTM for June in the group Nothing Better Than Reading. In October, it was BOTM in the group Ebook Miner, proving it was one of the most talked-about thrillers of 2014.

The second stand-alone thriller from the series, *The Church Murders*, was released April, 2015 to widespread critical and fan acclaim. *The Church Murders* became a bestseller in its categories throughout the summer and was nominated as Book of the Month in three different Goodreads groups.

Death of a Bride was the third Greek Island Mystery to be released. Released in April, 2016 it followed in the footsteps of its successful predecessors. From its first week in release it hit the number one spot for books set in Greece.

Murder On Display came out in 2017 and enriched the series.

Hotel Murder, the fifth and 'final' book in the series, followed in early 2018.

In 2018, his box set of mysteries became an international bestseller.

Luke Christodoulou has also ventured into 'children's book land' and released *24 Modernized Aesop Fables*, retelling old stories with new elements and settings. The book, also, features sections for parents, which include discussions, questions, games and activities.

In 2019, *Twelve Months of Murder* came out, his first collection of shorts.

His first novel outside of the Greek Island Mysteries collection came in 2020, maintaining his love for a Greek theme. A supernatural thrill ride with the name of *Beware of Greeks Bearing Gifts*.

Pandora's Box followed in 2021. A mind-twisting whodunit set in his favorite Greek town, the seaside resort of Parga. The following year saw the release of the highly anticipated *Achilles' Heel*.

His first YA murder mystery, *Senior Year Murders* was released in 2024, hitting the charts for young adult thrillers.

He is currently working on various projects (which he is secretive about).

He resides in Limassol, Cyprus with his loving wife, his chatty daughter and his super-energetic son.

Hobbies include travelling the Greek Islands discovering new food and possible murder sites for his stories. He also enjoys telling people that he 'kills people for a living'.